CHILDREN'S 21 day loan

OTHER PUFFIN BOOKS YOU MAY ENJOY

MOKI

MOKI

Grace Jackson Penney

Illustrated by Gil Miret

PUFFIN BOOKS

PUFFIN BOOKS

Published by the Penguin Group

Penguin Books USA Inc., 375 Hudson Street, New York, New York 10014, U.S.A.

Penguin Books Ltd, 27 Wrights Lane, London W8 5TZ, England

Penguin Books Australia Ltd, Ringwood, Victoria, Australia

Penguin Books Canada Ltd, 10 Alcorn Avenue, Toronto, Ontario, Canada M4V 3B2

Penguin Books (N.Z.) Ltd, 182-190 Wairau Road, Auckland 10, New Zealand

Penguin Books Ltd, Registered Offices: Harmondsworth, Middlesex, England

First published in the United States of America by Houghton Mifflin Company, 1960

Reprinted by arrangement with Houghton Mifflin Company

Published in Puffin Books, 1997

1 3 5 7 9 10 8 6 4 2

LIBRARY OF CONGRESS CATALOGING-IN-PUBLICATION DATA

Penney, Grace Jackson.

Moki / Grace Jackson Penney; illustrated by Gil Miret.

p. cm.

Summary: Ten-year-old Moki, a Cheyenne girl, wants to have the
adventures the boys in her tribe have.

ISBN 0-14-038430-8 (pbk.)

1. Cheyenne Indians—Juvenile fiction. [1. Cheyenne Indians—Fiction.
2. Indians of North America—Great Plains—Fiction. 3. Sex roles—Fiction.]
I. Miret, Gil, ill. II. Title.

PZ7.P3847Mo 1997 [Fic]—dc20 96-34478 CIP AC

Printed in the United States of America

Dedicated to

George

Michael

Stanley

and

Lynne

MOKI

THE SUN blazed down and the prairie sand was blistering hot to Moki's bare brown feet. She wanted to run fast as a rabbit down the trail to the creek where the other Cheyenne children were having a fish-catching, but Ha-Co-Dah was poking along as usual, taking his own good time.

Why did he have to be so slow? For that matter, why did he have to go everywhere that she did? He was too little to keep up with the others, and he always got tired and cross or went to sleep and had to be carried back to the tipi. She liked him, but a little brother could be a lot of trouble, sometimes.

Now he stopped to watch a lizard scurry into the scant shade of a scraggly bush. Moki hopped from one clump of dry grass to the next, pulling her foot up to cool it against her leg, waiting impatiently for

Ha-Co-Dah to catch up. Her soft deerskin dress seemed heavy and hot as she wiped her face on its fringed sleeve.

"Come on, Ha-Co-Dah!" she cried. "Can't you hurry at all? I don't see why they named you that. You certainly don't get around like any little grasshopper I ever saw. I'd change your name to Slow Turtle. That would fit you a lot better."

"My name's a good name." Ha-Co-Dah stuck out his lip defiantly. "My father gave me my name and I'll keep it. No girl can change it. One day I'll do a big thing, and an old man will ride about the camp, calling out my name for all to hear. *Then* you'll see who's a Slow Turtle."

"You and your big talk! It's not an easy thing to do a brave deed so that you are honored in the camp. You will see many winters' snows before the crier calls out your name!" Moki's tone was sharp. "Here, get on my back and I'll carry you." He'd be heavy, but at least they would get there faster. If only she were not so small and thin for her ten summers. Even Hogea was bigger than she was.

Her heavy black braids fell forward almost to the ground as she stooped to pick Ha-Co-Dah up, but he shoved her away so hard she nearly fell. "No, I won't! I'm not a baby on a cradleboard. I'm a big boy. I can walk."

"Well, come on then, if you're so big," Moki retorted. "Everybody else is already at the creek.

We're missing all the fun." She reached for his hand but he jerked away. He was a big boy indeed.

"Watch me, Moki! I can run fast. I can run as fast as a lizard!" He ran ahead, his short, fat legs churning up and down, small spurts of sand flying up behind his heels.

Soon they came to the canyon where tall cottonwoods made a cool shade against the burning noonday sun, and clear, shallow water ran over mossy brown stones. Moki half ran, half slid down the creek bank, Ha-Co-Dah close behind. Waiting for them there was Hogea, she who was called Little Mouse because she was a quiet one.

"Ho, Moki," she called. "We thought you weren't coming. What made you so late?"

"Ha-Co-Dah." Moki jerked her head toward her little brother, already down on his knees digging in the wet sand. "His legs are short. He can't run fast . . . besides, he has to stop and look at every little bug that crawls by."

Hogea pushed her braids back over her shoulders. "Why couldn't you leave him to sleep in the tipi?"

Moki gave a short laugh. "You wouldn't ask that if you had two brothers. He wanted to come, so I had to bring him along. Boys always get to do whatever they want to. I wish I were a boy, don't you?"

"Oh, I don't know." Hogea tilted her head to one

3

side, considering the matter. "I never thought much about it."

"Well, I have!" Moki said emphatically. It was one of the things she thought of most. Every time she saw her father look with pride at her brothers, every time she listened to stories of warriors' coups and heard the women's trills of applause for brave deeds, the wish grew bigger. It was like a strong fire burning in her, dying down sometimes but never going out. She gripped Hogea's arm. "You'll see! One day the camp crier will call out my name, and all the people will know that I, Moki, Little Woman, a Cheyenne girl, have done a big thing!"

Hogea gasped, her eyes big, "Moki! You can't! War honors are for men!"

Moki shut her lips tight. Hogea, the timid one, wouldn't understand. There was no use talking about it any more. She watched Ha-Co-Dah scooping out the wet sand. It wasn't fair that boys, just because they were boys, should get all the best of everything.

Hogea touched her hand. "Come on, Moki! Let's go down to the pool with the others. They've been working on the nets for a long time. If we don't hurry, we'll miss the fun. Come along, Little Grasshopper. Don't you want to see the fish-catching?"

The little boy jumped up and gave her one fat brown hand. Moki took the other and they trotted along the path, half swinging him between them,

4

until the little stream widened into a fine pool of clear water. Antelope Girl and some others were busy weaving tough willow branches into a mat. It looked nearly long enough to reach across the widest part of the pool. Moki and Hogea knelt to help with the weaving, and Ha-Co-Dah found a new place to dig in wet sand.

Out in the water, the big boys were driving stout poles down close together to make a sort of fence across the upper end of the pool. Moki knew them all. There was Red Feather, who was fat, and Tall Boy; and Hawk's Wing, whose father was the leader of the Kit Fox soldier society; and Little Wolf, Moki's older brother, and others.

All of a sudden Tall Boy gave Hawk's Wing a hard shove. Hawk's Wing grabbed Red Feather as he fell and they churned the water, wrestling. In an instant all the boys were rolling and tumbling, splashing the water like bears at play. The girls stopped working on the net to watch. Moki was still hot from walking in the sun. She would have liked to jump in the water, too.

The water fight didn't last long. Soon the boys were back at work, driving more poles. In a little time the fence was finished, and another slender pole set up in the middle of the pool. To this they tied a bit of meat, brought from camp. When everything was set up the boys waded out of the stream to let the water settle and clear.

"Last one to the sand bar is a short-legged Crow!" cried Red Feather, and away they all ran. Little Wolf, Moki's brother, was first to the sand bar. He threw himself full length on the warm yellow sand to rest in the sun. Nearly always in the races Little Wolf won, for his legs were long and his heart was strong. He was a tall boy, almost as tall as his father, Red Wolf, but slender and straight as a young pine. Already he walked among the others with something in his face that made them look to him as a leader.

Now, while Moki watched them, her hands still working at the net, she thought again of the fun in store for the boys. Soon there'd be feasts, and hunts, and war parties where they could count coup on the enemy and do brave deeds. There were all sorts of exciting things for the big boys. They would not have to carry wood, or scrape hides, or dig roots. A Cheyenne boy had a good time. Moki sighed and turned back to the net.

When the net was finished, it was time to gather wood and start the fire. They would need a good bed of hot coals to cook the fish. Moki's mouth watered at the thought of the crunchy brown fish they'd soon be eating. About the only thing better was buffalo tongue, which was served only at special feasts. Buffalo hump, roasted brown and juicy, was fine too, but fish, fresh caught and roasted by the creek on hot coals, was food fit for chiefs.

Finding wood was easy. There was plenty of dry driftwood along the creek, but getting the fire started was a bigger job. Antelope Girl spun the fire stick between her hands, faster and faster, until the dry powdered buffalo chip it rested on began to smoke. Of a sudden there was a tiny flame and Moki fed it with dry bits of grass. Next came small twigs, but she added them too fast, and the blaze almost died.

"Don't be so clumsy, Moki!" cried Antelope Girl. "Quick! Blow — blow on the fire! Give it some breath to live on."

Moki fed the little flame with more dry grass and blew on it gently so as not to drive the fire away. She added one small twig now, then two, and more dry grass and more tiny twigs; then larger ones. At last the fire was burning steadily and it was safe to pile larger sticks around it. Moki squatted back on her heels to watch it burn.

"You get in too much hurry," Antelope Girl said. "It takes time to make the fire live. Is not that so, Moki, my little one?" Antelope Girl always knew better than anyone just how to do everything, and she didn't mind telling about it. Moki felt her cheeks grow hot again, as much from the sting of Antelope Girl's words as from the heat of the fire.

"Ho, now!" Little Wolf called out. "The water is clearing up. Bring on the net, you girls. It is time to drive the fish."

The girls ran to get the net. Antelope Girl picked up one end. "Moki," she said, "you take the other end. You're too little to get out in deep water." Hogea took her place along the net with some of the other girls and they waded out into the water. Slowly they moved with the heavy willow net, until it reached across the whole width of the stream and there was no room for a fish to slip by on either side.

Then they began to wade upstream steadily, putting all of their weight on the upright poles to press the net down so the fish could not dart under it. Moki took one hand off the net to splash water on her face. The water was cold and felt good to her skin after the heat of the fire-making.

"Hang on to the net, Moki!" Antelope Girl called sharply from across the creek.

Up the stream the girls went, holding the heavy net against the pull of the current, until the net and the fence the boys had built made a small pen, with the bait pole in the middle. Now the trap was set.

They watched not saying a word. Then the bait-pole moved a little. The hair on the back of Moki's neck tingled. Something was after the bait. The pole moved, and moved again. Something was after the bait! The fish were here!

Now the big boys went into action. They slipped into the water, making no more ripples than so many otters. Slowly, slowly, they moved out near the center pole. Everybody waited, watching. In the silence the rasp of wood insects sounded strong and sharp. Moki held her breath until she thought her lungs would burst, her eyes intent on the boys closing in on the bait-pole.

Of a sudden, Red Feather plunged his arms into the water and came up with a twisting, flopping fish — a big one! "Here, throw it here!" yelled the girls on the bank. They scattered and then ran to capture the fish as it landed far back from the edge of the water.

Moki jumped up and down. Tall Boy made a dive and came up with another good fish to throw to the screaming girls. One of the other boys got a fish on his first try but it was a small one. It slipped out of his hands before he could throw it.

Little Wolf was luckier. He got an enormous fish on his first grab. It fought to get away. Gripping

the tail, he threw hard, but the fish fell, flipping and flopping wildly, close to the edge of the creek. It was almost back into the water when Ha-Co-Dah threw himself on it. The fish, almost as big as Ha-Co-Dah himself, put up a good fight to get away, but the little boy hung on and saved it. Moki yelled. Ha-Co-Dah had done a big thing. All the children praised him. Even Little Wolf said, "Very good, small brother."

Soon there was fish enough and it was time to prepare the feast. A good fire was burning and the girls fell to work, cleaning the fish. The boys rested, talking and laughing among themselves, waiting for the food. The air was full of the good rich smell of fish roasting on the glowing coals.

When the food was ready, they placed themselves in proper order for eating, just as the older people did at feasts in the camp. Little Wolf, as leader, took the place of honor as chief, with Red Feather on his left. He took a bit of fish and offered it to the spirits who rule the world, asking a blessing. Lifting the food toward the sky, he said, "Listeners-Above, eat," then toward the earth, saying, "Listeners-Under-the-Ground, eat." As he turned to the four directions, east and south, west and north, he said, "Spirits-Who-Live-in-the-Four-Parts-of-the-Earth, eat!" Then he placed the bit of fish on the ground beside the fire, and the feast began.

By the time the last brown crusty bite of fish was eaten the long afternoon was nearly over. A coolness rose from the water, and Moki's wet deerskin dress felt cold on her bare legs. Only the tops of the tallest cottonwoods were yellow with the rays of the setting sun. Soon darkness would come. Wet sand was put on the last red embers of the fire and everybody was ready to start back to the village.

The girls carried the sleepy little ones on their backs — even the proud Ha-Co-Dah, his drowsy head nodding against Moki's neck. He was heavy, and the trail seemed long and uphill all the way. The big boys fanned out on each side of the line of march. They were scouts, moving sharp-eyed and as silent as gray wolves, slipping from cover to cover, watching for the small movement, listening for the tiny sound that might mean an enemy nearby. Little Wolf and Tall Boy came last, in the place of honor, to guard the group from any danger behind.

It was gray dark when they came in sight of the home camp, but they could see people moving about among the tipis. An old man was riding slowly around the circle, calling out something. Perhaps he was announcing a feast or a dance, or he might be calling out the name of a man to be honored. Little Wolf pulled his scouts in close and led them around to the downwind side of the camp, to avoid being scented by the dogs.

Not a word was spoken. Little Wolf signaled

with a jerk of the head or a touch of the hand. Now they could smell the food in the cooking pots and hear the sound of people talking and still the dogs hadn't discovered them. Little Wolf was about to give the signal for his group to spring, yelling, into the camp circle when there was a clatter of hoofs and a whickering as the horse herd was brought in for the night. Every dog in the village set up a clamor and rushed out to defend the camp.

Little Wolf and the big boys ran to help with the horses while the girls and little children scattered to their tipis. Moki carried Ha-Co-Dah in and put him down on his bed without waking him. The sides of the tipi were rolled up and tied to let in the cool breeze that fanned the prairie grass at night. Ha-Co-Dah stirred and muttered in his sleep, but Moki patted him gently and he settled down again.

When she was sure that the little boy slept soundly, Moki went outside to feed her rabbit. "Eat your good grass, my friend," she said, stroking his soft fur. "I'm sorry I am so late feeding you — but, oh, Rabbit, the fish-catching was so much fun!" She bent closer to whisper in his ear: "I do wish I could have been one to catch a fish, but only the big boys do that . . ." Rabbit twitched his ear and stopped eating to look at her with his big soft eyes.

He'd been just a tiny baby rabbit when Red Wolf, Moki's father, brought him home to her. Grandfather made a little cage for him, and Moki fed and

13

watered him every day. At first he was wild and afraid, quivering when she touched him, but once he knew how much she loved him, he snuggled down contentedly in her arms. As he grew older Moki often let him out of the cage to play in the shade of the brush shelter beside the tipi.

He knew her voice, and usually came hopping when she called him, but sometimes he hid from her and she had to look and look for him. His flecked brown fur matched the grass so exactly. It was all a game for him. When Moki got close he would blink his eyes or twitch his long ears to attract her attention. Then she'd swoop him up and hug him close in her arms, laughing and scolding and calling him "Bad Rabbit!"

Running Deer, Moki's mother, broke into her thoughts by calling from the nearest lodge. "I am

here, my daughter, rubbing your grandmother's back
. . . Where is Little Grasshopper?"

Moki left her pet to stand just outside the tipi
door. "He went to sleep, coming home from the
creek. I put him on his bed."

The sides of her grandparents' tipi were not rolled
up. The prairie night winds grew cold to old bones
before the rising of the Morning Star, Grandfather
said. Moki's nose tingled with the sharp smell of the
medicine Mother was rubbing on Grandmother's
back. She sneezed and rubbed her nose.

Running Deer laughed softly. "What if you had
it rubbed all over your back? Then your nose
would surely tingle . . . And Grandmother's back
might not ache enough to need a rubbing if she had
had a little girl to help her with the dressing of the
hides."

Moki hung her head a little. Grandmother had
asked her to help, and she had meant to do it, too,
but she had forgotten and stayed away too long.
"I'm sorry, Grandmother," she said. "I meant to
come back and help you, truly I did . . . but it was
so much fun, the fish-catching. Let me tell
you . . ."

"Not tonight, Moki," her mother said, stepping
through the door of the tipi. "It's late, and Grandmother is tired. Wash yourself and go to bed. You
can tell me all about it tomorrow."

"But Mother!"

"It is the time for sleeping, my daughter." Running Deer's voice was gentle, but there was firmness in it too. "No more talking tonight. We may be going out for plums in the morning, so get your sleep now."

From down at the far end of the camp circle Moki could hear the throb of drums. One of the warrior societies was having a dance. Little Wolf and the older boys would be there, sitting quietly out of the firelight but watching every step, listening to the brave tales of war and danger told by the older men. That was the way they learned the history of their people and the ideals of courage and honor they would live by as young braves.

Moki stopped a moment to listen, wishing she could watch the dance too. Once, not too long ago, she had slipped away from the tipi and crept close to the firelight where the warriors danced. But she was shamed when Red Wolf, her father, had carried her home. "Little girls do not run about the camp at night, my daughter. Stay in the tipi with your mother." His voice had been sterner than she'd ever heard it, and Moki had cried, quietly, after he had returned to the dancing.

Now she looked up at the stars, shining so bright and clear, almost near enough to touch the tip of the tallest lodgepole. While she looked, one of the stars seemed to wink, and she said to herself, That star-person is watching. It seems friendly. I wonder if it is a little-girl star person. I will remember it and watch for it another night. Then she called out, very softly so as not to waken Ha-Co-Dah, "Good night, star person," and went inside to bed.

It was good to lie on the soft deerskin and look out at the stars and listen to the camp sounds. A cool breeze came over the prairie, and far away there was the sound of a flute. That would be one of the young men of the camp, perhaps Young Eagle, playing a love song. He would come closer and closer, playing ever more softly, until he would stand quite near the lodge of Spotted Fawn, the girl he was courting.

That was the custom. The girl would hear him, and she would know who it was, for each young man made his own flute and the sound of each was different. Perhaps, if the girl liked the young brave, she might come just outside the tipi door and talk to him. Moki had often seen young lovers, standing in the moonlight, whispering together. But now the flute's music was like the sound of falling waters far away, and the throb of the dance drums filled her ears, its fast beat setting the pace for the recounting of a young warrior's deeds of valor.

Moki's heart beat faster too, as she listened. How she wished she were there to watch the dancing and hear the tales of coups counted against a strong enemy! She shut her eyes tight, seeing in her mind the firelight glowing on the dark faces that

17

watched the dance of a fast-stepping brave.

The drums were beating slower now. That would be one of the very old men dancing, moving with great dignity as was fitting for a man of years and wisdom. It might be Grandfather Gray Hawk. He was one who could tell of many coups he had counted on enemies of his people, even to the touching of a Crow warrior inside his own tipi, and few there were who had ever lived to recount such a deed.

Grandfather's name had been called out in the camp many, many times. That Moki knew. She was proud of her grandfather and the honors he had won, and she thought of the boasting words she had spoken to Hogea, "One day the camp crier will call out my name and all the people will know that I have done a big thing." She was sorry she had said it, because Hogea couldn't understand, but somehow, sometime, she meant to make those words come true.

Thinking these thoughts, listening to the faraway sound of the flute and the slow throb of the drums, Moki fell asleep.

THE SOUND of falling waters was close now, so close that Moki could feel the cool droplets splashing on her face. Something bumped against the headrest of her bed and she awoke, startled. The tipi seemed full of moving figures in the dim dawn light, pushing and shoving, and the air was full of the sounds of their heavy breathing. Moki huddled down, afraid to move.

Were these dim-seen figures enemies, come into the camp to rob and kill? Her eyes strained to see better in the murky light. Where was her father? Moki bit her knuckles to keep from screaming.

Then she heard her father's deep voice, laughing. "That's right, young men. Get the lazybones out of bed. The sun will soon be up. Pull him out of there."

The breath came rushing back into Moki's lungs and she sat up in bed, laughing too. The "enemies" were Little Wolf's friends, come to rout him out because he slept too late, and the drops she had felt on her face were from the water they had thrown on him. The headrest of Moki's bed creaked as Tall Boy, yanking at Little Wolf, fell against it. Moki scrambled to get out of the way. The light was brighter now.

The boys swarmed over her brother's bed, trying to get a firm grip on him as he fought them off. At last Tall Boy and Turtle got his legs pinned down. Red Feather and Raven each held an arm. Laughing and shouting, they carried Little Wolf out of the tipi.

"Ho, here is the lazy one! He's out of bed before the sun is up, but not of his own doing," they called out for all the camp to hear. "This is the one who sat so late to watch the dancing and listen to the counting of coups by brave warriors. Now there are horses to be herded, and he sleeps late in his lodge."

Little Wolf fought free. He stood upright, panting. "I'm up now, my friends, and I thank you. It would shame me if the sun found me still in my bed. Come on, let's race to the creek. My legs are stiff from sleeping so long. Who can beat me to the water?"

With a shout they took up the challenge, racing down the trail to the creek for their morning bath.

That was the custom among the Cheyennes. Winter and summer, men and boys bathed themselves to start the new day. Women and girls, too, but only the men went into the stream in the early morning.

Moki brushed her hair carefully and tied her long black braids with deerskin thongs. Wide awake now, she went outside to the fireplace where her mother was getting ready to cook breakfast.

"Run down to the spring and get some living water," said Running Deer, handing Moki a water bag. There was water in the bag, but Moki poured it out on the ground. It had been standing in the tipi overnight, and so was dead water, not fit to use, even for washing.

Moki loved going to the spring in the early morning. The sun was just coming up and the air was cool and moist near the water. Ferns and vines grew in crevices around the spring, and there was the smell of dampness and of things growing, a cool and earthy smell, almost like the smell in a cave.

Someone, long ago, had made a little pool by piling stones across the stream below the spring. Here there was always water, even when there had been no rain in many moons. Cold, clear water, good for drinking and for cooking. Living water.

Moki knelt on the green moss beside the little pool. Three tiny fish darted through the water to hide under a small stone. She could see the pale gray-blue of the sky, reflected in the water, and her own small

21

round face, with its pointed chin. Her eyes looked back at her, big and dark like Ha-Co-Dah's, and the ends of her braids almost touched the water as she leaned closer to watch the fish.

"Chirr-ronk!" Moki jerked back at the sudden noise, ready to run. "Chirr-ronk!" Then Moki saw him, a big green-brown frog, squatting on a stone across the little pool. A big frog, so big he must be a very grandfather frog.

"Good morning, Frog." Moki spoke politely, as one should to a grandfather person. "I hope I am not disturbing you. May I fill my bucket from your pool?"

The big frog blinked his eyes, one at a time. His throat puffed out. "Chirr-rr-runkk!" he said, in answer.

"Ha-ho. Thank you!" Moki dipped her water bag in the stream while the frog watched her without blinking again. She looked back as she came to the turn in the path. He was still sitting there. She waved her hand to him.

Down the path she met Antelope Girl and Hogea. Moki waited while they filled their water bags and they all walked back to camp together.

"What are you going to do today," Hogea asked.

"I think we may go after plums," Moki said. She hoped Hogea would not mention her foolish boast about the honors she would one day win. Antelope Girl would only laugh at her. "That's what my mother said last night. What are you doing, Antelope Girl?"

"Oh, nothing very exciting." Antelope Girl shrugged. Nothing ever seemed exciting to her. "My grandmother is working on a robe for my father. She is putting a design on it showing how he counted coup on three Pawnees at the time of the Big Freezing Moon, last winter." She paused, then went on. "She said I might help her with some of the easy parts." She was proud of the beautiful embroidery her grandmother made with dyed porcupine quills, and inclined to boast about her own skill, also.

"I don't have anything special planned to do,"

Hogea said in her soft little voice. "I hope something really interesting comes up. What I'd really like to do is to go camping." She gave a little skip and some water splashed out of her container.

Moki thought about it, then shook her head. "I don't think I could go today . . . but it would be fun. Be sure to come by for me, if you do decide to go."

At home the fire was blazing away, and Running Deer had everything ready to cook. She was waiting for the water to mix with acorn meal to make the breakfast mush.

"What kept you so long, Moki?" she asked. "Has some mai-yun moved the spring farther away? Your father has taken Ha-Co-Dah to the creek, and Little Wolf has gone out with the horse herd, but they will all be back here for breakfast before it is ready."

Mother wasn't really scolding. It was just that she always had so much to do, and she wanted to have the food ready at the proper time. Soon her busy hands were stirring the cooking mush and turning the strips of meat on the hot stones. Moki was hungry. The food smelled so good she could hardly wait for it to be ready to eat. She was glad to see her father coming back from the creek with some of the other men of the camp.

Little Ha-Co-Dah came charging into the camp on a stick horse and pulled it up to a sudden stop just short of the cooking fire, his fat little body bouncing up and down as his play steed pranced under him. "Ho, horse! Ho!" he cried, trying to sound like a real pony rider. "Steady, horse! Ho!"

Red Wolf laid his hand on the little boy's shoulder. "It is not good to ride your war horse into the cooking place, my son. He might put his hoof into the kettle and spoil the breakfast." His voice and mouth were solemn, but Moki knew from his eyes that he was teasing Ha-Co-Dah.

"Let me take your horse, small brother," Moki said, feeling almost grown up as she went along with Father's joke. "I'll tie him back of the lodge. Then he can't get away and go back to the horse herd."

Ha-Co-Dah got off his stick horse and Moki dragged it around behind the tipi and propped it against one of the lodgepoles.

Little Wolf had come in when she came back to the cooking place. Red Wolf took a bit of the food and offered it to the Spirits-Who-Rule-the-Earth, then laid it beside the fire. Running Deer served them big bowls of acorn mush with a handful of fresh berries, and a piece of the good meat.

When the meal was over, Moki helped her mother clean the bowls and the cooking pots. She kept waiting for Running Deer to say something about going after plums, but when she got out her sewing kit and settled down to work on a shirt for Little Wolf, Moki knew that the plum-gathering was not to be that day.

"Hah-koa, my mother," she said at last, "I think I will go over and see how Grandmother is feeling this morning. She may need my hands to help her with something."

"That is good, my daughter," said Running Deer, cutting the bit of sinew she was using to sew up the sides of the shirt. "Tell her that I will have meat cooked for their supper this evening as well as our own."

Next door, under the brush shelter, Ha-Co-Dah and Red Wolf were talking with Grandfather Gray Hawk. Grandmother Doll Woman was inside the tipi, keeping out of sight of her son-in-law, for that was the custom among the Cheyennes. For a man to look at his wife's mother was to show a rudeness and lack of respect that would shock the camp. They never spoke, one to another, and each took great care not to meet the other face to face.

Moki went inside to speak to her. "Good morning, Nish-ki, my grandmother," she said. "I hope your back does not hurt you so much this morning."

"Thank you, Granddaughter, it is much better to-day." But Moki noticed that she leaned heavily on a stick when she moved about the lodge, putting things away in the rawhide storage boxes between the headrests of the beds.

"You rest, Grandmother," Moki said, patting the old woman's arm. "Let me make the beds and sweep the floor for you. I can do it."

She turned back the smooth soft skins on the beds and stirred the grass padding underneath to make it comfortable to sleep on. Tucking the skins down snug and smooth made the beds look very neat.

"Bring some water, Little Woman," Grandmother said when Moki had finished sweeping the floor with a brush broom. "If you sprinkle the floor it will keep down the dust and make it cooler, too." She hobbled over and took a pair of beautifully quilled moccasins from the rawhide case at the foot of her bed. "And while you're going out, will you take these moccasins to your father? They are not very nice, but perhaps he can wear them when the trail is muddy."

She put the moccasins into Moki's slim brown hands. "Run along with you now, my child. Give them to your father . . . and don't forget the water."

Moki picked up the water jar and left the tipi. When she gave the moccasins to her father he bowed his head in thanks. "Your grandmother is very kind," he said. "These are very fine moccasins, and my feet will walk lightly in them. It may be that they will carry me on good game trails when I go hunting tomorrow."

Red Wolf and little Ha-Co-Dah were watching Grandfather as he shaped an arrowhead. Already he had roughed out the point with quick sharp blows. Moki had watched him many times. It looked easy, just hitting one stone with another until the chips flew, but to hit just right so the shape would be right . . . that took a special knowing.

And it took more special knowing to put the sharp edges and the needle point on the arrowhead. Grandfather was on his knees, and the muscles in his arms stood out like knots in a rope as he put a sudden sharp pressure on the arrowhead with the tip of an antler. A tiny bit of flint flaked off, and Grandfather Gray Hawk leaned back on his heels and wiped his face with the back of his hand. The morning was already hot.

Ha-Co-Dah leaned back on his heels and wiped his hand across his face, too. He was trying to make an arrowhead too, and what a funny-shaped arrow-head it was! Moki laughed, and even Red Wolf smiled. The little boy looked from his arrowhead to the one Grandfather was making. "Nam-shin, my grandfather, how do you find the shape of the arrow-head in the stone?" he asked, frowning.

Moki laughed again, then stopped suddenly as Gray Hawk spoke. It was not good manners for a child to laugh when an old man was talking.

"There is a power, my grandson, that guides my hand when I strike the blows. That power I got from a master arrow maker, many, many summers ago, when I was a young man . . . much younger than your father."

Red Wolf nodded. "Your grandfather is known among all the people for the fine arrows he makes. He has indeed a great power."

"Tell me, Grandfather, how did you get this power?" Ha-Co-Dah asked, twisting around so that he could look up into the old man's face. "Could I learn to make good arrows too if I got that power?"

Grandfather put his hand gently on the little boy's head. "Do not be in too much hurry, my small one! It may be that when you are older you will be strong enough to make the sacrifices you must make to re-ceive power. Then the arrows you make will be good arrows."

He turned back to his work. Lips tight, he put pressure on the antler tip, and another tiny chip flaked off. They were silent, watching as the old man with a skillful twist of his wrists gave shape to the stone. After some time, Red Wolf walked away, going across to talk with some men who were sitting in the shade of a brush shelter on the far side of the camp.

Ha-Co-Dah started to follow him, then came back. He squatted on his heels, his back to Grandfather and Moki, busy with something — perhaps watching a bug crawling. Moki picked up a piece of flint, feeling the smoothness of the stone, turning it over and over in her fingers. She was thinking. When Grandfather laid down the antler tip, she spoke: "Nam-shin —" Then she stopped. It was a bold thing she was thinking. Gathering up her courage, she blurted, "Grandfather! Could I make an arrow?"

Grandfather jerked his head up and looked sternly at her. Moki felt her heart beat faster as he spoke! "That cannot be. It is not fitting that arrows should be made by a woman! Arrows are for war and for hunting, not for women's work. That is the way it has been since Sweet Medicine brought the sacred Medicine Arrows from the lodge of the mai-yum long and long ago." He lifted his hand in salute to the Spirits-Who-Rule-the-Earth, then turned back to his work. It was settled.

Moki blinked back the tears. There it was again.

30

Making arrows was something else a girl could not do, just because she was a girl. She threw the stone on the ground, and Grandfather looked up again.

"The mai-yun gave women their work, too, my granddaughter. Walk in the appointed way." His voice was kinder, but still firm. Wordlessly, she watched as he shaped the shoulder notches in the arrowhead. It took a long time to get them just the way he wanted them. Carefully, he selected a stick from several lying close at hand, then paused and pursed his lips. "Always keep this in mind, my granddaughter, a woman's feet do not fit a man's moccasins . . . but she does not go barefoot. She makes moccasins to fit her feet."

He held the stick up to his eyes, turning it slowly between his fingers. Sighting it carefully from end to end to make sure it was smooth and straight, he then took a piece of strong sinew and bound the arrowhead to the shaft, tying it securely. He cut and fastened the feathers to the shaft with glue, placing them just so. They had to be exactly right or the arrow wouldn't fly straight and true to its mark.

By now the sun was high and the little breeze that had cooled the early morning had gone to sleep. Grandfather stopped more and more often to wipe his face with his hand. Moki sat quietly, marking little trails in the sand with a twig, thinking of what Grandfather had said . . . what everybody always

31

said when she wanted to do something special. She jabbed hard and the stick broke with a sharp snap. Moki got to her feet.

Grandmother came out of the tipi, leaning on her stick. She looked surprised to see Moki. "Well, my granddaughter! Are you still here? I thought perhaps you had gone to the Big River to get the water for sprinkling the tipi floor."

The Big River was many days' march away across the open plain. Moki remembered standing on a high place, once, watching the brown waters of the Big River, rolling and rolling, as wide as a hundred creeks. While she looked a big tree came rushing down the river, swinging and dipping, with a little striped-faced animal clinging to it. She watched it out of sight around a big bend, and wondered where the little animal had gone, riding on the tree trunk.

But Grandmother was still talking, now. Moki dropped the twig she had been holding and ran over to pick up the water jar. "Grandmother, I'm sorry. I just forgot again."

Grandfather looked up from his arrow-making. The lines in his face made him look very old, and very wise. "It is not good to forget your work, my granddaughter. Something bad might happen to you." His voice was solemn. "Have you not heard of the young girl, long ago, who kept forgetting to do the things she was supposed to do? Her grandmother and her mother had to keep telling her over and over to do things she should have done without being told at all. At last a great owl came and carried her away and no one ever saw her again. When you hear the great owl calling in the night, you must remember the girl who always forgot!"

Moki shivered. Many times she had heard the strange call of the great owl in the night. Now she would always think of the girl who could not remember.

Quickly she picked up the water jar. "I'll go right now, Grandmother!"

But before she could turn away, Ha-Co-Dah jumped up and ran over to his grandfather. "Look, Grandfather!" he cried, his voice shrill with excitement. "Look at my arrow! I made it . . . I made a good arrow, Grandfather! Watch me throw it. See how straight it flies through the air!"

He threw the arrow with all his power. For a little, it went straight, then it turned sharply to one side and hit the water jar, knocking it out of Moki's hands. The jar fell to the ground and broke into many pieces.

There was a sudden sharp silence. Everything was so still that Moki could hear a baby crying far down at the other end of the camp circle. She was afraid to look at Grandfather. A water jar was a valuable thing. Most people used water bags made of rawhide or a buffalo paunch. Grandmother had made the pottery jar, and Moki knew just how much time and work and special skill it took to make it, Ha-Co-Dah had done a very bad thing. Grandfather would be very cross with him. Moki would not want to be in Ha-Co-Dah's moccasins.

"Bring me the arrow, Nishi," Grandfather said quietly. Moki looked at him as Ha-Co-Dah ran to pick up the arrow from the broken bits of pottery at her feet. Eyes big and dark, the little boy watched as Gray Hawk turned the arrow over and over in his hands, his face stern. At last he spoke, slowly and carefully. "Look, Grandson, this is not a good arrow. This arrow is bad medicine. Its power is bad."

Grandfather Gray Hawk took the little boy's hand and guided it along the rough edges of the clumsy point and down the crooked shaft. "You can see, Nishi, that this arrow could not fly true and straight because it is not built right. That is the way it is with people, my child. They cannot live true and straight if they are not taught right."

Grandfather stopped talking for a long moment, thinking, then he went on. "The Medicine Arrows were given to our people, long and long ago, so that we might know the straight way to go. It is not easy to live right, just as it is not easy to make a good arrow. It takes much patience and hard work . . . and a special power. These you will get, one day, if you seek the way and listen when the Wise Ones speak."

Ha-Co-Dah's hand looked very small in Grandfather's, and his brown little face was solemn as he looked up to the old man. Moki swallowed and blinked her eyes. It seemed as though she had been standing there a long, long time, watching the tall old man and the little boy, listening to the stern old voice.

"This is a very bad arrow. It has done a bad thing. It must be destroyed." Gray Hawk broke the clumsy arrow and threw the pieces away. Ha-Co-Dah's big eyes followed Grandfather's every move, but he made no sound. The old man turned back to the little boy. "How many summers have you seen, Little Grasshopper?"

Still Ha-Co-Dah didn't speak. He hadn't said a word since his arrow had shattered the water jar. Moki swallowed. Grandfather had asked a question. Someone must answer. She wet her dry lips with the tip of her tongue. "Five summers, Grandfather . . . He has seen only five summers, but I have seen ten."

The old man nodded, looking at Ha-Co-Dah. "Well, then, perhaps it is time for you to have a good throwing arrow, Grandson. You are old enough to learn to use it properly." Now Grandfather smiled at Grandmother. "This youngest grandchild of ours is growing up. Before too many summers have gone by he will be a man and a brave warrior . . . Yes, today I shall make him a good throwing arrow."

Ha-Co-Dah squared his small shoulders, standing as tall as he could stretch. To be a man and a brave

warrior was all a Cheyenne boy dreamed of. Grandmother brushed his hair away from his forehead and
looked into his eyes. "He is a good boy, this grandson of ours. We will be proud of him."

"But the water jar, Grandmother!" Moki blurted,
not able to hold back her indignation. Everybody
turned to look at her when she spoke. She stopped,
uneasily.

Ha-Co-Dah *had* broken the jar. Could it be that
he would not even be scolded? They spoke as if he
had done something good. If she, Moki, had done
this thing, would she have been treated the same
way? She didn't think so.

"I'm sorry I broke your jar, Grandmother. It was
a bad thing to do. I'm sorry, truly I am." Ha-Co-
Dah's voice was so low that Moki could hardly hear
what he said.

But Grandmother heard and patted his head. "The
jar is gone, my Little Grasshopper, and there is nothing to be done about that. But you shall go with us
when your sister and I go to the place of clay. You
can see then how a water jar is made. Not many
women among our people know how to make pottery
these days. It is a thing taught me many years ago by
my own grandmother, and I must give the knowing
to my granddaughter."

The old woman turned to go back into her tipi,
then she stopped and spoke to Moki: "Go now and
tell your mother that we are going to the place of

clay as soon as we have eaten . . . You do not need to say anything about the breaking of the water jar. Just tell her that you will be helping me."

"Come along now, Ha-Co-Dah!" Moki took his hand to get him started. She even gave it a little pull, in spite of herself. He was always so slow! "Let's get along home and tell our mother where we are going."

But Ha-Co-Dah pulled back, as usual. "I don't want to go home. I want to stay here and watch Grandfather some more," he said.

Grandfather shook his head. "Go along with your sister, Grandson . . . Moki, my little woman, ask your mother to send me a bundle of strong sinew. I have a thing in mind to do." He gave Ha-Co-Dah a playful spank and sent him scampering along the path. "A good throwing arrow takes time to make."

At home, Mother Running Deer gave Moki and Ha-Co-Dah food to eat and the bundle of sinew for Grandfather. Before they left, Ha-Co-Dah scampered around behind the tipi and mounted his stick horse, forgotten since breakfast time.

He galloped down the trail, leading the way as Moki and Grandmother came along more slowly. Grandmother Doll Woman still used her stick to steady her steps along the rough path, and Moki had to stop now and then to wait for her to rest a moment. Then she would have to hurry along to keep in sight of Ha-Co-Dah and his runaway stick horse.

The place of clay was across three low ridges and down in a deep ravine, where the wet-weather creek had cut a deep gash in the prairie and exposed a bed of yellow earth. Moki carried a pot of glue water

Grandmother had made by boiling bits of thick hide from a buffalo head in a clay-lined hole in the ground. Grandmother carried an old rawhide bag and some grease in a wooden bowl.

When they came to the ravine, Grandmother dug some of the hard yellow earth out of the bank with her stick, breaking it out in chunks. Filling the rawhide bag full of the clay, Grandmother hobbled down the ravine to a large flat stone half-buried in the earth, Moki and Ha-Co-Dah trotting along behind her.

"What are you going to do now, Grandmother?" Ha-Co-Dah wanted to know. He had never been to the place of clay before, and he wondered what Grandmother meant to do with the chunks of dirt.

The old woman leaned her stick against a tree and emptied the bag on the flat top of the rock. "We have to pound the clay into fine powder, Grandson," she said. "Get me a small stone, Moki; a round one, to beat it with."

Ha-Co-Dah came closer to watch as she worked. "But, Grandmother, why do you have to beat and pound it so hard?" he asked after awhile. "You won't have anything left but some dirt. Why don't you just pick up some dust out of the path, and save all that work?"

Grandmother smiled at the little boy. "Path dust won't do for this, Ha-Co-Dah. It takes a special kind of earth for pottery. And it has to be pounded fine and smooth, because if we leave any lumps in it or any little rocks, the jar will crack, or have holes in it, when it comes out of the baking in the firepit." She went on pounding and pounding the hard clay until every piece was broken into bits. Sifting the fine clay through her fingers, she sorted out the tiny pebbles and threw them away.

After a time, Grandmother handed Moki the pounding stone. "Here, Little Woman, you can help me. Rub the clay smooth now, while I rest my back."

Moki rubbed and rubbed the stone in the powdered clay. Ha-Co-Dah watched for a while and then ran off to play. Finally Moki stopped. "Is the clay not smooth enough now, Grandmother? Soon it will be all worn out." Her arms were getting very tired.

Grandmother took a pinch of the clay and rubbed it between her finger and thumb. "Not quite, Granddaughter . . . Here, feel it yourself. There are still some small grains in the clay. It has to be so soft and fine that a baby's breath would blow it away. It was that way that my grandmother taught me to pound the clay. Her grandmother's grandmother did it that way, long and long ago, when our people lived in earth lodges in the land near the big lakes. Have patience, Moki. Impatience makes a brittle pot."

"Why can't Ha-Co-Dah rub awhile, Grandmother?" Moki was tired of grinding the clay. "All he ever does is run and play . . ."

Grandmother looked shocked. "Let a boy help make pottery! Who ever heard of such a thing?" She pursed her lips, frowning. "Men do men's work. Women do women's work . . . That is the way it is, and that's the way it has to be."

Moki blew a wisp of hair that straggled into her eyes, and hit the stone harder. "I still don't see why . . ."

Grandmother tucked the wisp of hair back out of Moki's eyes. "Don't blow, Moki, you'll blow the clay away . . . It is because, long and long ago, when the mai-yun taught Sweet Medicine all the things the people needed to know, they set certain things to be done by men and certain other things to be done by women. It is not fitting that men make pots or quill robes. And it is not proper, either, for women to make bows or war shields. It is known that a war shield made by a woman would not have power to turn away a lance thrust by an enemy."

"And a jar made by a man would not hold water . . . is that what you mean?" Moki asked doubtfully.

Grandmother nodded. "That is true, my child . . . I think you may have the clay fine enough now." She sifted the powdered clay through her fingers, carefully going through all of it. "Yes, it is just right. Now pour a little of that gluey water into it . . . just a very little bit . . . slowly now . . . not too much. There, that's enough for now."

41

Grandmother carefully worked the clay into a sticky lump, adding more dry clay until it was a firm ball. The gnarled old hands kneaded and shaped it, using thumbs and a flattened stick to smooth it. The wet clay was tough enough to hold its shape, and Grandmother Doll Woman's hands were sure and skillful. Like Grandfather, when he made the arrows, she made her task look easy.

Ha-Co-Dah left his stick horse to graze and came to watch the pot take shape in Grandmother's hands. "Keep back, Little Grasshopper," the old woman said, not looking up from her work. "Don't come too close. A wet pot is easier to break than the one the arrow struck."

Ha-Co-Dah scraped the sand with his toe, not looking at his grandmother. "I'll stay back, Nish-ki," he said. "I just want to see it grow."

"Give me a little more water now, Moki . . . Just a tiny bit. Wait now, don't pour it so fast, a drop or two is enough." The pot was nearly finished. "You pounded the clay so fine and smooth that it is making a very nice jar."

Moki smiled, glad that she had had a part in making the water jar even if the rubbing was tiresome. Grandmother wet her hands in the gluey water and put the last smoothing touches on the jar. Then, being ever so careful, she set it in the sun to dry awhile.

"Come now, let's get the fire started." Grandmother was not one to waste time. They built a good hot fire in the firepit, and later, when it had burned down to glowing coals, the old woman greased the pot inside and out and put it carefully into the firepit.

Moki was worried. "But Grandmother! That hot fire will burn your jar . . . It will spoil it."

Grandmother went right on piling more and more wood on the fire. "A jar that can't live through the burning is no good, my granddaughter. You make the play dishes to last an afternoon. You do not burn them, and soon they crumble. The hot fire is like the trouble and the pain that comes to us as we live our lives. The person who comes through trouble is strong . . . and the jar will be strong . . . if it does not break."

Moki was not sure she understood what Grandmother meant, but she said no more, thinking about it as they fed the fire dried willow wood, because it made the hottest flame, until the pot was red-hot. After that, Grandmother allowed the fire to die, and a long time later she raked the ashes away from the pot so it could cool.

"Now we will soon know whether we have a good pot or not," she said. "While we are waiting, why don't you and Ha-Co-Dah go up the canyon and see if you can find some berries or plums?"

Ha-Co-Dah mounted his stick horse, ready to gallop away, but Grandmother shook her head at him. "I wouldn't ride my war horse, Grandson. Let him stay here with me, and eat grass."

Ha-Co-Dah stuck out his lip, not ready to leave his horse behind, but Moki took it from him, gently. "That's right, little brother," she echoed. "Leave your good pony here with Grandmother. There could be an enemy camp nearby, and you'd better scout along, on foot, to find out."

That did it. If he could be a scout, Ha-Co-Dah was willing enough to leave even his horse behind. Moki reached for his hand, but he jerked away and ran off up the ravine, darting from tree to tree.

Every now and then he dropped down to look closely at a broken twig or an animal track in the sand. "Keep behind me, Moki, and don't make any noise," he whispered. "I think there may be some people around this next bend. Let me go ahead . . . Watch me. I'll give you the sign if it is safe to come on."

He moved ahead while Moki waited. It was very quiet in the ravine. Ha-Co-Dah made no sound to disturb the stillness. Moki found herself holding her breath as she watched him slip closer and closer to the bend. What if there really were some people there? There couldn't be, of course. But what if there were? Crow or Pawnee hunters could be lurking there.

Ha-Co-Dah stood still, listening. Then he went on, but slower now. A step, then a pause to listen, and to look all around, then another slow, cautious step forward. Moki watched, not moving, herself.

Of a sudden a whistling whirr and a flutter of wings

right in Ha-Co-Dah's face made him leap backward. He stumbled over a root and fell down. Moki ran to him as he scrambled to his feet.

"Don't be afraid, small brother," she cried. "It's just a bird. Look at it. It's hurt, I think."

Ha-Co-Dah pushed her away angrily. "I'm not afraid. Ha-Co-Dah is never afraid . . . I knew it was a bird all the time. It just startled me, flying up in my face like that."

"Look at it," Moki cried. The bird was flying and falling, dragging one wing, making little crying sounds. "The poor little thing has a broken wing. Help me, Ha-Co-Dah. Let's catch it. We can take care of it and have it for a pet when it is well."

They ran and ran after the bird, but always it managed to keep out of their hands; fluttering, falling, moving away from the path, but never quite letting them get their hands on it.

"It's harder to catch than that big fish yesterday at the pool," Moki panted.

"But I did catch the fish, didn't I?" Ha-Co-Dah declared stoutly. "I will catch this bird, too."

"Oh, let it go!" Moki said at last, out of breath and tired of chasing the bird. "Let's go on up the ravine and look for berries. I'm thirsty."

Together they turned back to the path. Then the strangest thing happened. The bird flew around in front of them and began to act crippled again, dragging its wing, hopping along, making little cheeping cries. Moki laughed. Now she knew what it was all about.

"Of course! It's a mother dove. She must have a nest here somewhere. That's why she's acting like that. She wants us to chase her, so we won't see her nest. Come on, Ha-Co-Dah. Let's see if we can find it."

Now that they knew it was there, it wasn't hard to locate the nest, perched insecurely on the branch of a little tree, but it was empty. "That's a strange thing," Moki said, puzzled. "Why would that mother bird try to lead us away from an empty nest? Keep looking, Little Grasshopper. I believe there is something here, somewhere, she doesn't want us to see."

Then Moki saw them. It was just a flash of a beady eye that she caught sight of first. But when she looked more carefully she could see the two baby birds, lying so still on the ground. Their feathers were marked just like the sticks and grass around them, and if one little bird had not blinked his eye she might not have seen them at all. "Ssh, Ha-Co-Dah! Be quiet. Do not scare the small ones. Look, there by the old log. Can you see the baby doves?"

"I see them . . . I see them!" whispered Ha-Co-Dah, dancing with excitement. Moki reached out to hold him back. "Let me go, sister. I want to catch the little birds."

"No, no, little brother. It would be a bad thing to catch the baby birds. They are not big enough to eat by themselves and they will die if you take them away from their mother. She must feed them, you know."

The old bird flew at them desperately, almost striking Moki in the face with her wing, trying to drive them away from her babies. "Come on, Ha-Co-Dah," Moki insisted. "Let's go on away and leave them alone. That brave mother bird will beat herself to pieces if we don't get away from them. She has a strong heart to protect her young ones."

A little farther up the ravine they found a few low bushes with some big ripe berries. Ha-Co-Dah and Moki ate some, quickly, and the sweet rich juice was as welcome as fresh spring water. They picked all they could hold in their hands and carried them back to where Grandmother was waiting for them in the shade of a big willow tree.

"Shut your eyes, Grandmother," Ha-Co-Dah cried. "Shut your eyes and open your mouth, and I'll give you something very good."

Grandmother chuckled as she shut her eyes tight and lifted her wrinkled brown face. Ha-Co-Dah dropped three of the biggest, juiciest berries into her mouth. "Now eat, Grandmother," he said, watching to see how she liked them.

Grandmother smacked her lips, relishing the sweet berries. "Ha-ho, thank you, my grandson! I was getting so thirsty that my tongue felt like the sole of a very old moccasin."

Moki laughed to think of a person's tongue feeling like that. "We found a fine bush with many good berries. We ate some and brought the rest to you." Moki poured all of her berries into Grandmother's lap.

They told her about the mother dove and the two little birds. "Look, Grandmother, this is the way the old mother bird did." Ha-Co-Dah flapped his arms up and down and ran, hopping along the ground, making cheeping noises like the bird.

"She was trying to lead us away from her young ones," Moki said. "We found them . . . two of them, hiding in the grass."

"Yes, and I wanted to bring the baby birds back with me," Ha-Co-Dah said, still resentful, "but Moki made me go away and leave them there."

"That was the right thing to do, Nishi," Grandmother nodded. "It is not good to take birds so young. They are not good for eating, so small, and if you let them grow they will make a dinner for someone, one of these days."

Grandmother took up a little fine white sand and rubbed her fingers with it to clean them of the berry juice. "Give me your hand, Moki," she said. "Help me to get up. I'm stiff from sitting here so long. It is time we started back to the village."

"Bring Grandmother her walking stick, little brother. And you'd better get your horse up and ready to go." Moki helped brush the dust from

Grandmother's buckskin dress. It was a pretty dress, beaded and fringed.

"Come on, children. Let's see how our pot is looking, now that it is cool."

It was a very good pot, Grandmother said, smiling at Moki after she had turned it this way and that, looking it over carefully for any flaw it might have. "Even my grandmother would have been proud of this water jar. Taking time to pound the clay so fine was the important thing, Granddaughter. You see how smooth and even the pot is now? It would not have been so if you had left your work too soon. You may carry it back, if you will walk carefully."

Moki wanted to run fast, back to the camp, and show the new pot to her mother. It was hard to go along slowly, watching every step so as not to stumble. Ha-Co-Dah rode ahead on his stick horse, galloping like the wind, to pull up to a plunging stop before the tipi door.

"Nah-koa, my mother!" he called, his eyes black and shining with excitement. "Come and see the new pot that Grandmother and Moki have made."

Running Deer had been sewing a shirt for Little Wolf. Now she fastened the straps on the parfleche and put the rawhide box between the headrests of the beds. She stepped outside into the glow of the sunset and waited for her mother and Moki to come closer.

She looked at the new pot very carefully, feeling along the smooth curves of its sides. "This is truly a fine water jar, my daughter. Your grandmother will teach you to make pottery as good as they made in the old days when our people lived along the big lakes."

All around the camp the women were coming out of the tipis, starting their cooking fires to make supper. Soon there was a tempting smell of cooking meat in the air and a bustling about among the lodges as parties of men came in from the hunt, bringing what game they had managed to kill. Some of the big girls led the pack horses down to the creek for water, hurrying to get there and back before the sun was entirely out of sight across the prairie.

Suddenly there came a loud call from a hilltop not far away to the west. Everybody stopped to watch as a young man stood on the highest place, signaling with his robe. Once, twice, four times he made his signals to tell the camp that his scouting party had found a herd of buffalo—a large herd, by the signs.

Word was brought to the Old Man Chief in charge of the camp. He named the hunt leaders and sent the camp crier to ride about the circle, announcing that everything was to be made ready for a hunt the next morning. Men looked to their bows and checked their supplies of arrows. Women hurried the suppers along, and young boys raced out to bring the horse herd in close for the night. Moki was excited. The whole camp had not moved out on a big buffalo hunt in many moons.

After supper there was a gathering of the men at their soldier society lodges to hold their special ceremonies to make the buffalo easy to kill. Old Owl Man, who had a special power, opened his medicine bundle and passed the sacred objects from it four times through the smoke of white sage sprinkled on live coals. Then he prayed to the Spirits-Who-Rule-the-Earth, and again passed the objects through the smoke four times. This ceremony was to make the buffalo blind as the owl in the daytime, so they would not see the hunters as they came upon them.

Another medicine man did special ceremonies to make the buffalo unable to scent the hunters as they came close. And all the time the medicine drums kept up their steady beating to bring the blessings of the spirits on the hunt, that there might be food in the village when the strong cold came.

Long before the sun was up, the camp was ready to move out on the hunt. Far out in front rode the hunters, each man leading his best-running horse to save it for the chase when the buffalo were sighted. Red Wolf was there with his soldier band. He was one of those named to lead the hunt. The spotted horse that Little Wolf rode belonged to his grandfather. He had trouble keeping the eager pony under control so that he would be fresh for the running, for Little Wolf had no second horse.

Grandfather did not go out on hunts any more. Time was when he was a mighty hunter and his lodge was full of meat and fine new robes. Time was when he gave great feasts for his warrior society. Now he was old. No longer was his arm strong enough to thrust a lance point deep into the life-center of the buffalo. But Red Wolf too was a good hunter, and he kept their tipis well supplied with food.

The women of the camp led pack animals and carried their sharp skinning knives to dress out the buffalo the men would kill. Boys too young for the hunting ran along beside them, eager to share the fun.

But it was not all fun for the men. Hunting was their work, the way they got food for their families, and the buffalo hunt was the most important one of all. They ate the meat, made their tipis and much of their clothing from the skins. Buffalo robes kept them warm in the moon of the strong cold. Many of the tools they used were made from the bones and horns of the great beasts.

In the cool of the early morning, Moki walked along with her mother and the other women and girls, all of them hurrying to keep in sight of the hunters. Ha-Co-Dah was perched on the big, gentle pack horse led by Running Deer. Little Grasshopper drummed his heels on the pony's fat sides and yelled shrilly at him, but the old horse only twitched one ear forward and back, lazily, and kept plodding along at the same steady pace.

Coming into more broken country where a little hill blocked their way, Red Wolf raised his bow above his head, to signal that they were near the place. All the men got down from their horses, and the women hobbled the ponies so that they could not run away. Working fast, but silently, the men laid aside all of their clothes except breechclout and moccasins and tied their braids together behind their backs. They

wanted nothing to get in their way when they started to shoot the buffalo.

Red Wolf and Yellow Bull, head man of the Kit Foxes, worked their way to the top of the little hill and looked down into the valley on the other side. Moki waited with the others, watching the scouts closely; no one made a sound. When they came back down, all the men gathered in close to hear Red Wolf's low-voiced report.

"The valley is a good place for a surround," he said. He squatted on his heels and drew lines in the sand with a little stick. "Here is where we are now. The buffalo are over here. There are trees and bushes to hide us from them as we come in from the east, and the wind will be in our faces. To the west the valley narrows sharply . . . a few men can guard that end." He looked up from his marking and pointed with the stick. "You, Black Elk, take your men around to the far side of the valley and wait behind the ridge. You men of the Crazy Dog society, go down into the valley below the herd. Take care not to let the old buffalo chief know you are there."

He stood up and motioned to another group. "You men go to the narrow end . . . The rest of you wait here. When everyone is in place we will ride in upon the buffalo from all sides at the same time. If the mai-yun take pity on us today there will be feasting and new robes in every lodge from this day's work."

Yellow Bull nodded. "That is true, friend. The

buffalo in the valley are as many as the leaves of a cottonwood tree. Sharpen your skinning knives, you women. They will have much work to do today."

The men rode off to take their places for the surround. The women tied their pack horses and got ready to take care of the meat when the hunt was over. The place was as busy and as silent as an anthill, and the children kept out of the way of the women. Moki took Ha-Co-Dah and crept up to the top of the little hill and found a place where they could look down through the branches of a scrub-oak bush and see what was going on in the valley below.

It was a beautiful little valley, level and smooth. The great shaggy buffalo had their noses buried in the good green grass. Only the old buffalo chief was looking around, standing guard over his herd.

Ha-Co-Dah wriggled with excitement. His elbow moved a pebble and sent it rattling down the hill in front of them. The old buffalo shook his head and pawed the ground. Moki gripped Ha-Co-Dah's arm. "Sh! Be quiet! If the old buffalo chief hears a noise he will stampede the herd."

But the old bull must not have heard. He stood at the edge of the herd, taller and bigger than the others, keeping his watch while they ate. When a breeze came he snuffled the air noisily, then shook his great body from nose to tail. Off to one side, two young bulls began to fight. One shouldered into the other, and with a rumbling bellow the other charged him.

57

Grumbling and grunting, they hooked and butted heads. The rest of the herd went on eating, paying no attention, and the noise of the fighters covered any sounds the hunters might have made as they moved into position for the charge.

Suddenly, from all sides, the hard-riding hunters charged down upon the grazing herd. "Look, Ha-Co-Dah! Look!" Moki screamed. "There's our brother on his spotted pony! See how fast he rides!"

All the women and children were standing on top of the hill now. Ha-Co-Dah jumped up and down; he was wild with excitement. "I see him!" he cried. "I see Little Wolf! What's he doing now, Moki? What's he doing now?"

"He's getting close so he can shoot the buffalo in the right spot to bring him down. Watch how near he comes to that big bull!" Moki clenched her hands into tight fists. How she wished she were riding down there! Her heart pounded as she watched the racing hunters.

Now Little Wolf rode beside a plunging buffalo, his knees gripping his pony's sides, his arrow taut in the bow, another arrow clenched in his teeth, ready for a second fast shot. All about him the grunting, bellowing beasts were running from the hunters who surrounded them. No time now to see what others were doing, Little Wolf's eyes were fixed on the galloping bull. As the wise spotted pony swerved in he let fly the arrow. The buffalo plunged on, not slack-

ening its pace. Little Wolf shot it again, then reached over his shoulder for a third arrow. But there was no need to shoot again, for of a sudden the great beast swerved, stumbled and went down. The wave of snorting buffalo, yelling men and racing horses swept around and over him.

Ahead was a young bull. Little Wolf raced on toward it. Suddenly the bull stopped short, turned sharply to one side and Little Wolf swept past him, not able to turn the spotted pony fast enough to get into position for a shot. Another hunter closed in and sent a deadly arrow into the young bull.

Moki and Ha-Co-Dah could not see Little Wolf any more in the mass of bellowing buffalo and yelling hunters. Every man was shooting as fast as he could fit an arrow to his bow. Dead buffalo lay all around the valley, and only a few of the herd broke through the ring of hunters and scrambled up the far hillside to get away.

The hunters pulled their heaving horses to a stop, then, and the women and children ran down to count the buffalo they had taken, Ha-Co-Dah scrambling along down the hill behind Moki. A tall hunter saw the little boy and called out to him.

"Come here, small one. Let me show you where to shoot a buffalo to kill it with one shot." Ha-Co-Dah ran to him, and the hunter pointed to the place right behind the shoulder. "There is the life-spot, little brother." Pulling his arrow out of the great beast, he marked Ha-Co-Dah's face with a little of the dark buffalo blood. "There, that is to bring you the good hunting when you are a man."

Little Wolf with his spotted pony was standing beside a fallen buffalo. Red Wolf came up to him just as Moki and Ha-Co-Dah ran up. "My son, I see you have made a kill," he said, pride strong in his voice. "It is a fine, fat bull. You have done well, my son."

"Ha-ho, thank you, my father." Little Wolf's eyes showed his pleasure at his father's words, but his face was sober. "I hope the meat was not made tough by the running. It took the second arrow to bring him down. I must practice shooting so that I can shoot straighter, next time."

Red Wolf laid his hand on Little Wolf's shoulder. "You have done a big thing. Now gather up your arrows, and take care to clean them well . . . and you, Moki, help your mother take care of the meat.

60

Tell her, my daughter, that we have another hunter in our lodge."

All around the valley the men were dressing out buffalo, leaving the skin stretched out on the ground under the carcass. The women cut the meat up into large sections and loaded it on their pack horses. For a feast, the prized portion was the tongue, boiled until it was tender and juicy. Buffalo fat, roasted until it was crisp and brown and crunchy, was a relished tidbit for Cheyenne children.

It was late afternoon and their shadows stretched long before them as the Cheyennes returned to camp with every horse loaded with good buffalo meat and hides. In front of their tipi, Red Wolf sent for a poor old man who had no strong sons to do his hunting for him. He had been a good hunter who kept his lodge well stocked with meat when he was younger, but the cold of many winters had stiffened his fingers and dimmed his eyes.

When the old man came Red Wolf said to him, with pride plainly showing in his face, "Look, my friend. See this horse and the load of good meat he carries. The meat is from the fat young bull . . . the first buffalo killed by my son, Little Wolf. Hear my words, my friends. This horse and this meat I give to you, in honor of my son, who will be a mighty hunter in the camp."

Running Deer and Moki made the sound of the trill, as was the custom when a man did a thing worthy of honor. Little Wolf stood silently beside his father, his eyes modestly looking at the ground.

The old man took the pony and led him around the camp circle, calling out in a loud voice that Little Wolf, young son of Red Wolf, had killed his first buffalo, and that Red Wolf had given a good horse loaded with meat to him, a poor man. So it was that all the camp knew what Little Wolf had done, and the people talked about it and spoke his name in praise. Moki was full of pride in her brother. It was a big thing to have one's name called out before all the camp.

Little Wolf took the spotted pony he had ridden in the hunt down to the creek. Moki helped him wash the horse carefully, and brush his coat until it glistened in the late evening sun. Then he led the pony back to Grandfather's lodge.

"My grandfather, I give you my thanks for letting me ride this fast horse," Little Wolf said. "He has a strong heart. Right into the thick of the buffalo herd he carried me so that I was able to make a good shot." He put out his hand, with the halter rope. "I bring him back to you, with my thanks."

Grandfather Gray Hawk's wrinkled old hands closed over Little Wolf's. He shook his head. "No, my grandson. This horse is no longer mine. Because you rode him well, and because today you killed your first buffalo, I give this horse to you. You will ride him on many hunts and war trails. May he always bring you good fortune, as he has today."

Grandmother brought out a pair of moccasins, quite the finest that Moki had ever seen. They were decorated with porcupine quills, dyed and worked into a pattern that had medicine power to lead the feet into the straight way. These she put into Little Wolf's hands with a little speech praising him for his success in the hunt that day.

Little Wolf thanked them for their presents. Moki ran on ahead to tell her mother about them. Ha-Co-Dah listened, his black eyes gleaming. "You will see, my sister. One day I shall kill a giant buffalo . . . the biggest buffalo bull in the whole world. Then my father will give away *two* horses, and all the camp will hear my name."

He was boasting, but Moki knew that he truly would one day hear his praises spoken by all the people. She wished that she could do something, anything, to make her father as proud of her as he was of Little Wolf, and the wishing was like a heavy stone in her heart.

She wandered away to feed her rabbit. While he ate she held him close in her arms, stroking his soft silky fur. Darkness was walking along over the prairie as the red sunset faded in the west.

"Rabbit, do you grieve that you are not a strong, brave animal?" Moki whispered to him. "Do you like being . . . just a rabbit?"

The rabbit stopped nibbling an instant and looked

at her, one ear tilted forward, the other dropped back. He looked so funny and solemn that she laughed and hugged him so tightly that he struggled to get free. She popped him back into his cage with a final pat. "But you're such a sweet rabbit, and I love you just as you are! Don't ever, ever change into a big strong animal."

That night Moki dreamed that she was riding a fast horse in a surging herd of buffalo, trying to get into position to shoot. Just as she started to let fly an arrow, the bowstring caught in her hair and the great buffalo bull changed into a giant rabbit. She could hear all the people laughing as she turned her horse and rode away from the hunt, ashamed.

FOR MANY DAYS after the hunt the Cheyenne camp was as busy as an anthill that has been stepped on by a buffalo cow. Everybody was working. There was no time for visiting from tipi to tipi. No time for feasting and dancing. No time for playing the wheel and stick game.

Because the mai-yun had taken pity on them and allowed so many buffalo to be taken, all the people had to work together, and quickly, to take care of the meat and hides so that nothing should be wasted. The men built extra drying racks and helped the women cut the meat into thin strips. Soon every tipi was surrounded by racks strung with good strong meat, drying fast in the hot, dry prairie wind.

The children had a very important part in all this busy time. They had to keep the camp dogs away from the tempting meat. Let a hungry dog so much as trot near the drying racks and a whooping, yelling Cheyenne boy was after him, pelting him with pebbles.

Ha-Co-Dah was the busiest little boy in all the camp. He kept his trusty stick horse at hand all the time, ready to charge out and drive away the dog enemies. Soon Old One Eye, Ha-Co-Dah's special pet, learned that it was better to stay well away from the tipi, but the half-grown pups could not believe that none of that fine-smelling meat was for them.

This year, Moki was too big for playing the dog-chasing game. She was busy helping Running Deer and Grandmother Doll Woman hang the strips of meat. By the time the last of the strips were up those hung first were dry and ready for putting away in storage boxes for the winter. She could do that, but she was not big enough to make pemmican. Squatting on her heels, she watched while her mother pounded and pounded the good lean meat until it was as fine as acorn meal. Grandmother brought chokecherries, dried and pounded too and mixed them with the pounded meat.

The smell of the pemmican made Moki's mouth water. "Nah-koa, could I just taste it?" Moki asked.

Running Deer smiled. "Just a very small taste, my daughter. You know how important it is to keep a good supply of pemmican for the winter."

Moki did know that. Warriors always carried a small pouch of pemmican with them when they went out on raids and war parties, for a handful of rich, nourishing pemmican would keep a man strong for days. But it smelled so good that she could not resist taking a tiny taste while she helped pack it away in the rawhide storage boxes.

Finally, after all the meat was cared for, the women started to dress the hides. Grandmother and Running Deer had four great hides to tan. It wasn't easy to get the heavy buffalo hide stretched out on the ground, hair side down. Moki helped drive the pegs that held it tight while Grandmother scraped it with her flesher, to take off every scrap of meat that might still be left on it. Then she thinned it even, — so that it would take the tanning mixture of liver and brains, grease and soapweed that she rubbed into the hide.

She was making a robe, so she left all the hair on the hide. Usually the Cheyennes wore their robes with the hair side out, but when the strong cold came they turned the warm woolly hair side next to their bodies. Moki liked to snuggle under a warm buffalo robe in her bed and listen to Winter Man's icy wind blowing shrill around the tipi. It was good to be safe and warm inside the lodge when Winter Man was angry.

Grandmother was humming to herself as she scraped the hide, paying no attention to Moki, kneeling on the grass nearby. It didn't look too hard, the fleshing. "Let me try it, Grandmother," Moki said, and when Grandmother didn't answer she pulled at her dress. "Grandmother, aren't you tired? Let me help with the fleshing."

Grandmother shook her head, without stopping her work. "The flesher is sharp, Little Woman. It would be easy to cut a hole and spoil the robe. You must learn to use the flesher on little things before you work on a buffalo hide."

The old woman stood up to rest her back, holding the flesher in her wrinkled brown hand. "Look, Moki. See these marks? This is the mark my mother made on this flesher when my grandmother gave it to me. That was the year that I married your grandfather. I had seen the cherries ripen ten and seven times."

Moki looked into her grandmother's face, trying to imagine her as a laughing girl, listening to the sound of the courting flute, knowing from its music that it was Gray Hawk calling. Grandmother rubbed the flesher with her thumb, a faraway look in her eyes.

"Ai-ee," she sighed at last, "that was long ago. Many marks have been scratched on this flesher since then. This long mark . . . it is for the year my first son was born, and this one is for your mother, my oldest daughter."

Moki looked at the row of scratches. So many of them, and each mark telling of a whole long year. "This tiny mark, my grandmother. It is short, but it is deep. What does that mean?" She touched the worn old flesher with the tip of her finger.

Grandmother's eyes darkened with long-remembered sorrow. "That is a bad mark, a mark of trouble, my granddaughter. It stands for a time of sickness. Many people died in the camp that winter. Sorrow was in every lodge. My mother died . . . and my first-born son. I tell you, we were glad to see the Hoositoo, the Taking-It-Home storm that meant the end of that winter."

She stood, looking backward into time long gone, her face deep lined with the trail of years and sorrow. Moki didn't ask any more questions. It was not good to stir old memories. She was glad when Grandmother bent again to her work, saying sharply, "Here I've been talking and talking, Moki, and the hide is getting too dry to handle. You'd better take the water jar and bring some water from the spring."

Moki didn't want to go to the spring again. Already today she had made trip after trip, and the water jar got heavier and the path longer every time. But Cheyenne children obeyed their elders, always, and Moki trudged away, thinking of Grandmother and the old flesher with its long row of marks. Somehow, it made the long years of Grandmother's living like something Moki had known herself . . . as real as last winter's throat-hurting, and the growing of the young leaves in the springtime.

On the way she met Antelope Girl and Hogea,

who were bringing water back to their mothers.

Antelope Girl set her water jar on the ground and pushed her hair away from her face. "Ai-ee," she said, "that old jar gets bigger and heavier every trip. I'm getting tired of running back and forth so many times. You'd think they'd take the hides down to the creek. It would save a lot of water-carrying." She sounded cross.

"That thirsty wind dries out the hides faster than we can get water to them, Grandmother says." Moki swung the empty jar in her hand, hoping that Antelope Girl would notice it.

"Isn't that a new water jar you have there?" It was Hogea who asked. Antelope Girl was too full of her own concerns really to notice anything else. Hogea was different. "It looks like a very fine jar. Let me see it. Did your grandmother make it?"

Moki held it out to her. "Yes, my grandmother made it . . . but she let me help her. Run your fingers over it, Hogea. Feel how smooth it is. This water jar will never leak!"

Antelope Girl was looking at Moki with new interest. "You really helped make this fine new water jar, Moki? Could you make one all by yourself, now?"

Moki wanted to say yes she could. She wanted them to think she had the power to do this thing. Antelope Girl was older and taller than she was, and Moki always had the feeling of trying to keep up with her, and never succeeding. She opened her mouth to say yes, but something made her shake her head. "No . . . No, but I did help. I pounded the clay so nice and smooth . . ."

Antelope Girl tossed her head. "Anybody could pound clay. I thought you had really done something. Come on, Hogea. I've got to get this water back to my mother." She picked up her water container and started away. Then she stopped and looked back over her shoulder at Moki. "Did I tell you that *my* grandmother is quilling another robe? This will be three times ten robes my grandmother has quilled."

She didn't have to say any more. Moki knew that the quilling of thirty robes brought a woman honors as proud as those of a warrior who had counted coups. Always she would take a chief place in the gatherings of the women. Not many women ever quilled so many robes. Antelope Girl had a right to boast about her grandmother. Only a woman who had made and decorated a tipi entirely by herself was more honored.

Moki felt herself small in the eyes of her friends, and her cheeks burned at the sound of Antelope Girl's laughing. She was still standing there in the path, looking after them, when Ha-Co-Dah came riding up on his stick horse.

"Ho, Moki, the slow one! Will you be all day bringing the water? Grandmother says the hide is getting stiff and dry. Bring the water quickly." He turned his horse sharply about and galloped back toward the camp.

When Moki got back with her water jar, there was company in the tipi. Two Crows, the mother of Spotted Fawn, was there, visiting with Grandmother and Mother. Two Crows was a large woman, very fat, but her daughter was as slim and graceful as a young deer. Two Crows was talking. She always talked a lot. Spotted Fawn was quiet, and shy, and her voice was soft. Moki listened wide-eyed to the women's talk.

"It was yesterday that Young Eagle returned from a raid." Two Crows clasped her plump hands. "A stalwart young man he is, that Young Eagle. A taker of many horses. He brings honor to his father's lodge."

Moki's mother and grandmother made soft sounds of agreeing. "A good son he is," they said. Moki thought of Young Eagle, the tall young brave, slender and straight as a pine tree. In the shooting matches his arrow found the center of the target from a farther distance than any other young man's.

Two Crows was still talking. "A brave warrior he is, and good at taking horses. Do you know how many horses he brought back from that last raid?" Twice she held out her hands, palms outward, fingers spread wide, and again three fingers. "Twenty-three good horses he took from the Pawnee herd."

She stopped, waiting for the effect to sink in on her listeners, watching them with her bright black eyes, deep-set in her fat cheeks. Grandmother and Mother Running Deer gave the little trill of applause for a brave deed.

Two Crows pursed her lips and nodded her head with great satisfaction. "I speak with a straight tongue. Twenty-three there were, and seven of them war horses. I counted them this morning when I found them tied outside our lodge. That was before the father of Young Eagle came to ask that our daughter, Spotted Fawn, be given to his son as wife."

"There will be a wedding, then?" Moki's mother asked, while Moki wriggled with excitement. She loved a wedding. There would be feasts and games and special storytelling, and everybody would be hurrying about getting presents ready for the young couple. Wedding times were fun times in the camp.

Two Crows nodded her head slowly, her lower lip sticking out. Moki thought she looked a little bit like a frog, sitting there on the ground. "There may be a wedding. There is no objection to the young man, but the brother who has been given charge of Spotted Fawn is away with a hunting party. He must be the one who gives the answer. So I led the horses back to Young Eagle. If he likes, he can present them again when Spotted Fawn's brother returns."

She hoisted herself heavily to her feet, puffing.

"Will you help with the lodge-making? The hides have been tanned, and the poles are cut and peeled. I have a great bundle of strong sinew ready for the sewing, and Buffalo Woman has said that she will cut and lay out the skins. Come to my tipi at the fourth rising of the sun. A feast will be ready."

Grandmother Doll Woman and Running Deer were happy to accept her invitation to the lodge-making. It was an honor to be asked. Moki would have liked to go, too, but she knew there was no use to ask. Only women who were known to be skillful in sewing and of a pleasant nature were asked to help make a tipi for a bride. It would be Moki's place to stay at home, taking care of Ha-Co-Dah, for children running about would be in the way. Perhaps they could go to the feast, after the lodge was finished and an old woman, long and happily married, had walked across it, to bring happiness to those who would make it their first home.

When Two Crows had gone away Grandmother returned to fleshing the buffalo hide, and Mother to her sewing. Moki watched her mother. It looked easy, just punching tiny holes with the sharp awl, threading the strong sinew through the two pieces of deerskin, and pulling it smooth. Mother's slim brown hands worked swiftly, making strong, even stitches. It would be a handsome shirt. Father Red Wolf would be proud to wear it.

Moki put out a finger to feel of the soft deerskin.

"One day I will make a shirt for my father," she said, half to herself.

Mother smiled. "You do have big thoughts, for such a small person," she said. "Perhaps you will make a war shield, too, my brave daughter."

Moki caught her breath, shocked. "A war shield! No war shield made by a girl could stop the arrows of the enemy! My father would be killed!"

Then she saw her mother's face and knew that Running Deer was teasing her again. Moki laughed a little, too, but she didn't like it much. Always she was too little, or she couldn't do something because she was a girl. One day she'd find a way to do something . . . something special. Then her father would look at her with pride in his face, and all the camp would speak her name.

It seemed a very long time to Moki before Elk Horn, the brother of Spotted Fawn, returned from the far mountains where he had been hunting with a party of young men. Young Eagle again left his rich offering of twenty-three good horses outside her father's tipi.

At a family council Elk Horn listened to the words of Young Eagle's father, spoken after the proper ceremonial smoking of the pipe. After he had returned to his own lodge there was a time of silence in the tipi, then the brother of Spotted Fawn spoke, addressing his words to his uncle since it was not fitting that a brother speak directly to his sister after he was seven winters old.

"Is it the wish of our sister that she enter Young Eagle's lodge, to be his wife?"

Spotted Fawn kept her eyes on her hands, clasped

before her. Her voice came as a shy whisper: "Tell my brother . . . it is my wish."

So the giving of presents from one family to the other and to the poor people of the camp and the feasting and dancing and the singing of songs went on for the proper number of days. At last came the day when Young Eagle and Spotted Fawn, dressed as became a bride in a fine new dress of whitest, softest deerskin, had eaten together from the same bowl in the new lodge made for them, and there was a new family in the camp circle.

To the children of the camp it was a time for playing games, for running races, and for eating until they could eat no more. Ha-Co-Dah and his hard-riding fellows gave their stick horses no rest as they galloped up and down among the lodges.

But Moki, feeling somehow lonely and left out of things in the midst of the excitement she had been looking forward to so eagerly, kept as close to her mother as her shadow. Whatever Mother Running Deer did, Moki was beside her, watching, trying to help . . . until at last her mother said wearily, "My daughter, is there no game that little girls like to play? Why do you not go with the others to play by the stream."

So Moki wandered off, down to the creek where Hogea and some of the others played in the cool shade. Little Wolf and Tall Boy had gone into the prairie toward the rising of the sun, early that morning. Moki had watched them filling their quivers with arrows, testing the strength of their bows. They would be coming back before the darkness covered the prairie, perhaps bringing with them a fat young antelope or some prairie chickens to fill the cooking pots.

If they got an antelope, Moki knew that her father would be much pleased. It took great cunning to shoot the wary, swift-running antelope, and to bring one in showed hunting skill that could make a man proud of his son.

The girls were playing with a ball. Standing in a circle, arms linked together, they took turns bouncing the deerskin ball, stuffed with buffalo hair, on their feet. Each girl kept the ball as long as she could keep it going by hitting it with the top of her foot. When she missed it the next girl in the circle took her turn. It was a fast game, one played mostly in the wintertime, and it took skill and practice to keep the ball going for long.

Moki watched while two girls kicked the ball, losing it after several bounces. When it came Antelope Girl's turn she tossed her braids back over her shoulders and kicked the ball faster and more times than the other two together had been able to do. When at last she missed, Moki took her place in the circle next to Hogea, third in line from Antelope Girl.

She kept the ball for only three bounces before she let it fall to the ground. Antelope Girl laughed, and Moki felt her ears grow hot and water filled her eyes so that she could scarcely see the ball she was scrambling for.

"Ho, I'm tired of this baby game," Antelope Girl said, turning away. "None of you play it well enough to keep it interesting . . . Let's go swing on the grapevine down on the big sycamore . . . and you, Moki, bring my ball along, if you can hang on to it better with your hands than you do with your foot."

It was in Moki's mind to drop the ball and run away somewhere alone, but Hogea put her arm around her and whispered, "Don't cry about it, my friend. Everybody misses the ball sometimes."

Moki rubbed her eyes, trying to laugh. "I think I must have something in my eye. Perhaps that is why I missed so quickly."

Hogea squeezed her arm. "Of course! Now, come on! Last one to the swing is a poky mud turtle."

It was a good race, and Moki was not the last to reach the big grapevine looping down from the syca-more tree. A good, free feeling came to Moki, swing-ing high, with the rush of air blowing away the last of the hurt from Antelope Girl's laughing.

As she swung, leaning far back, looking up and up into the thick-growing green leaves of the vine, Moki saw a gray squirrel. He was sitting up on a limb with his bushy tail curved up behind him, watching them intently with beady bright eyes. He had something in his paws, and while she watched, swinging, he nibbled at it. Then, of a sudden, as if someone had called him, with a flirt of his tail he was gone, running swiftly down the limb and across on a vine to the next tree.

While she waited for the others to take their turns on the swing, Moki lay on her back, hands under her head, her eyes open but not seeing the treetops above, not even hearing the talk of the girls as they played.

In her mind she was following the game trail with Little Wolf and Tall Boy, seeing them stalking the fleet antelope herd. They would be circling widely, to come up close on the downwind side, slipping like shadows from one bit of cover to another. She held her breath, waiting for Little Wolf to fit his arrow to the bow and let it fly. The nearest antelope jumped twice, then fell, with the arrow in his side, as the rest of the herd sped away.

It was enough. Little Wolf would turn back to camp, bearing his kill across his shoulders. Moki could see him in her mind's eye, dropping the antelope at his father's feet, and the pride in Red Wolf's voice as he said, "You have done well, my son."

Moki stirred, pulling her hands out from under her head, feeling the tingling in her arms from lying there so still so long. Her eyes blinked, then came to a focus on the treetop above her. On the vine, high overhead, hung clusters of purple grapes, full and round and rich with ripe, sweet juice.

As she looked at them a thought took shape in

Moki's mind. She couldn't go out and kill an antelope, that she knew, but she could climb up there and get some of those good grapes. These she could take to her father. He would know she had climbed high to reach them, and she would see pride in his eyes as he looked at her . . . Moki, the little one, who had never done anything to make him proud.

The other girls stopped their playing as she started to climb the big sycamore. "What are you doing, Moki?" one asked, and Antelope Girl said, with a little smile, "Are you chasing the gray squirrel, little one?"

Moki didn't answer. It took all her breath and strength to pull herself up the big trunk. The scaling bark of the sycamore peeled off in her hands, and the rough edges scraped her knees as she inched upward until she could reach the first stout limb. Once there, she rested and wiped her face with the back of her hand, breathing hard, as if she had been running a long way very fast.

Below her the girls, led by Antelope Girl, pretended to be dogs, barking at the foot of the tree as if they had Old Striped Face, the raccoon, treed. Moki looked up. The ripe grapes hung high overhead, and she wondered if she could ever reach them. Maybe she had better get down while she could.

But she did want those grapes for her father . . . and the only way to get them was to climb up there where they hung, purple against the blue sky. So she

kept inching her way upward, pulling herself from
limb to limb, afraid to look down again, until the
thick clustering grapes were close at hand.

Holding fast to the branch overhead she reached
out as far as she could stretch toward the biggest,
ripest bunch. Her fingers touched the grapes but she
couldn't quite grasp them. She shifted her hold on
the limb above and reached out farther.

"Be careful, Moki!" It was Hogea calling shrilly
from below. "Watch yourself or you'll fall!"

In spite of herself, Moki looked down and her
throat tightened to keep back a scream. It was so far
to the ground! The limb she was standing on bent
under her weight and broke. She grabbed for a hand-
hold to save herself. Not knowing how she did it,
she got back to the tree trunk, clutching it with all
her strength, the fear making a quivering in her stomach.

For a time there was no sound from the girls below, shocked into quiet by her near fall. Moki could
hear only her own heart pounding and pounding like
a dance drum, loud in her ears.

"Come down, Moki!" Hogea's voice was a breathless shriek. "Come down from there!"

Moki forced herself to open her eyes. A quick
look down and down to the ground made a stronger
fear to lock her arms to the tree. She couldn't move.
The smell of the sycamore bark against her face was
sharp and burning to her nose, and her mouth was as

dry as milkweed down. She tried to swallow, to call out, but no sound came.

Moki never knew how long it was until her father came up into the tree to bring her down. When she felt his strong hands holding her safe she dropped her arms, stiff and numb from gripping the tree, and leaned against him, shaking like the young cottonwood in a strong wind. She turned her face against the buckskin of his shirt, not wanting to look into his face for shame.

On the ground again, Father Red Wolf rubbed Moki's arms and hands to make the pain go away, and Hogea brought water from the stream to wash her face and to cool her dry throat. Antelope Girl and the others stood by, staring and whispering.

Men and women from the camp came to see why Red Wolf had been called from the wheel and stick game so suddenly. "It is nothing, my friends," he told them. "My daughter climbed too high in the sycamore tree. That is all. Perhaps she thought she was a gray squirrel, to run about the branches."

Moki covered her face with her arms. She did not want to see the smiles on their faces as they went back to their own concerns. But she could hear Ha-Co-Dah saying, "Tree-climbing is not a thing for girls, is it, my father?"

And Antelope Girl said loudly, "Come on, all of you! Let's not stand around here any longer. It's my turn at the swing. Give me a big push, Hogea. I want to swing high!"

Moki and her father were alone at the foot of the big tree. For a long time there was silence. Moki felt small, small and miserable. She didn't know what to say to her father. He couldn't possibly understand *why* she had gone up into the tree. There was no use trying to tell him. If only he would go like the others, and leave her alone.

At last Red Wolf stood up and lifted Moki in his arms. Setting her gently on her feet, he said, "Wipe the tears from your eyes, little daughter. Everyone tries to climb too high, sometimes. Let us go back to camp. Your mother will be wondering where we are."

THE DAYS that followed the tree-climbing were days for keeping close to home, for staying away from Antelope Girl and the others. Even in the home tipi Moki kept out of the way as much as possible. She was so quiet and listless that Mother Running Deer asked Grandmother to give Moki some special tea to make her feel better. But the bad feeling that Moki had was not something that Grandmother's medicine could cure. It was just the knowing that she had done a foolish, dangerous thing and had embarrassed her father, and time was the only medicine to cure the hurting of that.

When late summer came at last to the Cheyenne camp, it brought a new restlessness to all the people along with the blue haze that hung over the prairie at dawn and twilight. There had been no rain for many moons, and everywhere the grass was dry and brittle.

Buffalo wallows that earlier had held clear pools of water now were sun-baked mud flats. Every morning, when Moki went very early to the spring for water, she saw tracks of deer and skunks, of squirrels and the tiny hand prints of Old Striped-Face the raccoon, come there to drink since water was scarce on the prairie.

Men rode out early to hunt and came in late, often long after the sun had left the sky. Red Wolf went south with a war party, after far-ranging scouts brought word of a band of Comanches with a big horse herd and few warriors. They were gone for ten sleeps, and when they returned, the blanket signals told of success.

But the loss of two brave warriors made Red Wolf's face stern, even as the captured herd was driven into camp. He got down off his horse and walked silently into the lodge of the Old Man Chief, where the Wise Ones sat in council. There was a stillness throughout the camp, too, except for the high-crying wails of the women whose men had not returned.

For Moki it was more than ever a time to be quiet and listen, and the sound of the women's sorrow was like a heavy burden dragging on her shoulders. She wanted to wail with them, but it would not be fitting.

All night long the drums sounded, and the chants for those dead in battle. Moki slept and woke, and slept again with the sad sounds of mourning in her ears. Lying in her bed, she searched the sky, but the pattern of the stars was different and she could not find the friendly star-person. Moki wondered if she would ever see that star again, and the thought that it had gone away for good made her feel more lonely than ever she had felt before.

With the morning light, and when she could bear the silence and the sound of the women's crying no longer, Moki took her rabbit out of his little cage and carried him in her arms down to the spring, taking comfort from the feel of his soft fur against her cheek. After a time she let him down and smiled to see how greedily he nibbled the tender green plants near the water.

The coolness and the scent of green growing things felt good after the sun and dry-dust smell of the camp. Lying on her stomach on a flat rock at the edge of the little spring pool, she let her fingers dangle in the cold, clear water, feeling the tug of the small current, half listening to the birds singing and the small talking sounds of the stream as it tumbled over a rock ledge nearby.

She may have slept then, or was dreaming, half awake, for the sun was higher when she had a sudden feeling that something was near . . . some danger threatening. Perhaps it was the sudden silence that alerted her.

Quickly, she looked up. There, across the little pool, yellow eyes gleamed. Tiny flecks of white froth glistened around a long muzzle.

It was a coyote skulking in the shadows. Moki's heart pounded so loud she thought he must surely hear it, but he wasn't watching her. His yellow eyes were fixed on something behind her. He ran his tongue over his slavering lips and crouched to spring.

She knew it had to be her rabbit he was staring at. With one swift motion she leaped to her feet, scooping up Rabbit, and ran for the camp, not daring to look behind her, sure she could hear the pad of the coyote's feet running after her.

Red Wolf was leaving the tipi as she ran in, breathless. He stopped to listen as she blurted, "There's a terrible coyote at the spring . . . He was after my rabbit! Please, Father, go down there and kill him!"

But her father had no time right then. "The coyote will go away," he said. "Now I must finish up the business of the war party. There is sorrow in the camp, for men have died. It is not a time for small things." He patted her head, kindly, but turning away at the same time. "Take care of your rabbit yourself, small daughter. I have many things I must do, now."

Red Wolf strode across the camp circle. He was a Wearer-of-the-Sash, one who staked himself to the ground with his lance in battle, pledged to conquer the enemy or die where he stood. Tales of his bravery and power were told around the campfire. It was not good to have bothered such a one about a thing so small. It was right that he should walk away.

But the coyote . . . something had to be done about him. He might come right into camp and get her rabbit. He looked fierce enough to do that. Moki searched for Little Wolf or Grandfather. Neither of them was to be found. But there was a stout club beside Little Wolf's bed. Moki tucked Rabbit into his cage and fastened the door securely. He crouched, watching her, his nose twitching.

"Don't be afraid, my rabbit," Moki said, patting his head. "I won't ever, ever let anything hurt you!" And Rabbit hopped over into a corner and snuggled down to sleep. A cage is a good place for a rabbit, Moki thought. Nothing could harm him there . . . But suppose the coyote did come after him . . . would the cage protect him? It didn't look so very strong, really.

Setting her jaw grimly, Moki went back inside the lodge to get Little Wolf's club. It was heavy, but she could handle it, somehow. Down the path to the spring she went again, keeping a sharp watch on all sides, expecting the coyote to spring at her from behind every bush.

If he did come at her, she meant to fight him with that club . . . to drive him away from the camp so Rabbit would be safe. But the birds were singing again, and the only sign of the fierce coyote was his big paw prints in the soft earth beside the pool.

Moki ran back to camp, hardly feeling the weight of the heavy club, so glad was she that the coyote had gone away. A sense of being somehow bigger and stronger than she ever had felt before took hold of her. She had, after all, been brave enough to go out by herself, to drive away the danger that threatened her pet.

Mother Running Deer was waiting for her, calling out as she came near, "Come along, my daughter. Today we shall go for the cherries."

It was only a small party of women and girls who were going out after cherries that day, but they would bring back all they could gather and divide them with those in whose tipis sorrow lodged. There was not the laughing and the singing usual among the women on this walk across the prairie. The talk was quiet, and turned on serious things.

"It is a sad thing that two of our men lost their lives in the raid against the Comanches," one said.

"Ai-ee! A sad thing it is!" another agreed, shaking her head in pity. "And one is the only hunter for his wife and three young children. His old mother, too, looked to him for food and had no other son."

"The other one, Bear Claw, has a tall young son who will, perhaps, swing to the pole and become a warrior when the Arrows are renewed, at the next Sun Dance," Running Deer said as the women stopped to rest.

"I have heard that he does well in the hunt, that one," another woman said, taking the cradleboard from her back and checking the small one sleeping there. "It is good that there is a son in the lodge. There will be no hunger there."

"Other hunters will share their meat. Our friend's children will not go hungry while there is food in the camp. Always the old people and the children without fathers are to be fed, as Sweet Medicine taught the people, long and long ago." It was the oldest woman who spoke, one who was much older than Grandmother Doll Woman, and the others listened with respect to her words.

"Let us go on," Running Deer said, standing up. "Or there will be no cherries to share with them, or to make pemmican for our warriors, either."

Walking along, the women spoke of the Sun Dance. Runners had come into camp not long before, summoning the band to a coming together of the whole tribe at the time of the next big moon. Sand Crane it was who had pledged to renew the Arrows that the favor of the mai-yun might be restored to the Cheyennes. It was said that the mai-yun had been displeased with the people since they had lost a battle with the Crows at the time of the last Big Freezing Moon.

Moki walked close beside her mother, listening to the words of the women, one of them an aunt of Sand Crane who had gone with the young men on the warpath.

She told how the whole tribe was camped along the Big River, and certain young men went out in the time of heavy snow to take horses from a strong Crow village, far down the river. These were headstrong young men, new members of the Kit Foxes warrior society, eager to do a big thing that their names might be known among the people.

These men asked the War Chief for permission to go out, and he sent them to the Keeper-of-the-Arrows, that the proper ceremonials might be performed. Certain things happened that led the Keeper-of-the-Arrows to the knowledge that it was not good to go out against the Crows at that time. This knowledge he gave to the young men of the Kit Foxes, and they bowed their heads before the old man, as if they accepted his words.

But during the day and into the night, one by one they slipped out of the camp and met at a spot they had agreed upon, to go against the Crow village in spite of the warning.

"I have heard how they slipped up very close to the Crow village, the third night, while Hoemaha, the Winter Man, blew sleet into their faces as if to drive them away. But they were stubborn, and they pushed on, leaving one man to guard their own horses. There was no light in the sleeping village, and no scouts watched the horses that were tied close among the tipis, for safekeeping." Sand Crane's aunt stopped to take a pebble out of her moccasin, then went on, telling of the raid.

"There was not a sound in the camp, and Sand

Crane, my nephew, and the others were just about to take away the best of the Crow horses when of a sudden a very strange thing happened." She paused, and there was that in her voice that made a shiver go up Moki's back. She was glad the sun was shining and her mother was near enough to touch.

"Yes, my friends, a very strange thing happened. A thing no one had ever seen before . . . A big gray wolf come right into the middle of the Crow camp and ran across the open place in the center, howling and howling as he ran. All the camp dogs came charging out, making a terrible noise, to chase the wolf. Crow warriors poured out of every tipi with their lances and war clubs in their hands. The horses began to snort and rear, squealing and blowing, and the Cheyenne young men had to run for their lives, back to their own horses, empty handed . . . and some bearing lance wounds in their bodies."

There was a clicking of tongues and a shaking of heads among the women. "And now, against the Comanches, we have lost two of our brave ones," they said. "Truly, the mai-yun must be greatly displeased with our people. It is a time for the renewing of the Arrows, and for the ceremonies of purification."

"The Sun Dance will turn the thoughts of the people into the straight way," Moki's mother spoke softly. "Their hearts will be made new, and all of us will walk a better road when the prayers and sacrifices have been made. It is not good to turn away from the counsel of the Wise Ones."

When they came to the place where the cherries hung ripe on the branches of small trees, the women spread their robes on the ground and shook the trees until the cherries pelted down like hailstones in a summer storm. Some were so ripe that the falling split their skins and the sweet juice ran out, smelling rich and good in the warm sun.

Yellowjackets and hornets were quick to gather around to join the feast, buzzing and humming like flies. They were so busy sucking up the sticky juice

that they had no time for stinging, even when Moki brushed one of them off a fine big cherry and popped it into her own mouth. He buzzed angrily, but quickly settled on another fruit.

The mother held a sweet ripe cherry to her baby's lips and his little tongue sucked at it greedily. He ducked his head and wrinkled his nose, showing two white teeth as he reached out to bring the juicy fruit back to his mouth.

Moki clapped her hands. "Let's call his name Yellowjacket," she said. "He's after the cherries like a little yellowjacket, so let's call him that!"

The mother laughed a little, but shook her head. "This one has a name his uncle gave him. It is a good name, and will not be changed until he is old enough to earn another one for himself." The others laughed, too, at the boldness of a small girl who would think to give a child a name.

Moki felt her cheeks grow hot with shame at the women's laughing, but she looked down at the ground without saying anything else aloud. To herself she said, stubbornly, I shall call him Yellowjacket just the same. I don't care what name his uncle gave him!

It was a small thing, the laughing, but it spoiled the good feeling she had had since the morning when she had mustered courage enough to go after the fierce coyote with a club. It made her feel small again, and she was glad when they turned back toward home. As soon as they had the cherries spread on racks to dry in the hot sun all the women went down to the creek to wash themselves and their robes.

Mother Running Deer washed Moki's hair with the crushed roots of the soapweed, and fanned it gently until it was dry and soft and glistened in the sunlight like a crow's wing. Carefully she brushed and braided it in two long braids, wrapping the ends with soft deerskin, tied with thongs.

That night not even the drums and songs of mourning could keep Moki awake long after her head touched the pillow filled with fragrant pine needles, and no dreams of honor came to disturb her sleeping.

MOURNING for the warriors lost in the raid against the Comanches continued for four days and four nights. Drums beat without ceasing, and the necessary tasks of the camp were done quietly and without joy. Men did not go out to hunt, and the warrior societies held ceremonies in their lodges. Moki and the other children of the camp stayed close to their own tipis, playing no noisy games.

The tall young son of Bear Claw, the warrior who was struck down by a Comanche war lance, came before the Wise Ones with gifts, asking for a teacher who would help him prepare for the rites that would make him a warrior. Hour after hour he sat with bowed head before them, listening as the Wise Ones spoke to him of the things a Cheyenne warrior must understand. They were preparing him to bear the pain and suffering he must endure to prove himself a man, when he should swing to the pole at the time of the Sun Dance.

It was a time of sober thinking among all the older boys. Their faces were grim as they hurled their lances and shot their arrows in practice. Little Wolf, never one to do much talking, came and went about the lodge like a shadow, so still and silent.

At last he broke his long, brooding silence, speaking to his father as they sat alone in the tipi very early one morning, not knowing that Moki was just outside. His voice was low, but there was that in the sound of it that made Moki hold her breath to listen.

"My father, I would go into the hills for a dreaming."

A dreaming! He would go alone into a high place, to think and to pray to the Spirits-Who-Rule-the-Earth, to wait without food and water for days, if need be, until a vision should come to him to show him the road of his life . . . to reveal to him the name . . . the very secret and personal name that was his alone, never to be spoken to anyone . . . and the medicine power which would be his for strength and courage.

Now this starving time, this time for seeking the Way, was come to her brother as it did to all Cheyenne boys; and Moki sat, small and quiet, on the ground outside the tipi, clenching her hands to stop their shaking. She hoped the others could not hear the sound of her heart, pounding at the brave thought that came to her as she listened. She knew she should not be there at all. It was not fitting that a girl should hear the instructions given to one who was going out for a dreaming.

But she *was* hearing! Straining not to miss a word, she listened to the solemn, slow-paced words of her father. She did not dare to look again at them, for fear that her looking might bring their eyes to see her. When at last they left the tipi and walked away, the breath went out of her throat in a rush, and she felt as if she had been running a long time. But the brave thought, wild and daring, was still big in her mind!

Just as soon as her father and Little Wolf were out of sight, she jumped to her feet. She would do it! She could, and she would! Now, quickly, while everyone was away from the tipi! Oh, it was a brave deed she would do. A big thing. Antelope Girl would not laugh at her and call her "little one," after this. Her mind churned up all the long-buried hurts; when Father Red Wolf had no time to be bothered with her, when the women had laughed when she wanted to give the baby a new name, when she couldn't help with the fleshing because she was too little, and she couldn't make an arrow because she was a girl!

Never, never, from the beginning of time, had a

Cheyenne girl gone out for a dreaming; but she, Moki, would go out. She would fast, and pray, and do all things needful, just as her father had so carefully instructed Little Wolf. Then she would wait and the mai-yun would take pity on her and she, Moki, the little one, would be given a vision.

She felt big and strong, and excitement lent wings to her feet as she ran, cutting across the prairie, staying well away from the trail where someone might see her and stop her. Well she knew that a little Cheyenne girl was not allowed to run about the prairie alone. Any party who found her would take her back to her mother's tipi, so she was careful to stay out of sight. She knew where she would go. She had seen a little hill, piled high with a jumble of broken rocks, when she went with her mother to gather cherries. There she would go for her dreaming!

The morning was still cool when she reached the rocky knob. It was higher than it had looked from the place of the cherries, and it took longer to climb to the top. Moki remembered the delicious juice of the ripe cherries, but she turned her thoughts away, swallowing to bring moisture to her drying throat. There was no time for thinking of food or ripe, juicy cherries. She was here for a special purpose.

Standing on the highest point, stretching herself up as tall as she could, she lifted her face to the morning sky in prayer to the Listeners-Above. Then she lay full length on the ground and prayed to the Listeners-Under-the-Earth. After a time, standing, she faced east, then south; west, and, finally, north, praying aloud to the Spirits-Who-Live-in-the-Four-Parts-of-the-Earth that they might take pity on her, the first Cheyenne girl to come to them this way, and show her the right road.

Then she settled herself to wait. It was pleasant there on the little hill, high above the prairie. She could look away and away, far to the very edge of the earth, it seemed. Overhead a buzzard swung in slow, swooping circles against the dazzling blue of the cloudless sky. Moki spread her arms and swung about, pretending she was a bird too, lifted on the breath of the wind, sailing and sailing above the rolling prairie. But a rough stone hurt her bare foot, and she sat down to rub it.

Into her mind came the legend she had heard long ago, about the lazy, funny little man, Wihio, and his ride on a buzzard. She could hear again the laughing of the people as the storyteller told of him falling to earth again, tipped off of the buzzard's broad back, and limping back to camp with no one to believe that he had actually flown through the air. Poor Wihio, she thought, a man is not supposed to fly. He should have known that.

Moki shaded her eyes against the sun glare and looked back in the direction of the camp. Far across the prairie she saw some men riding out — a small party, perhaps as many as the fingers of one hand, going out to hunt, or to take horses. A thought crossed her mind. They might be looking for her! Quickly she huddled down among the rocks so that their sharp eyes might not see her.

For a long time she lay there, still and very quiet, to be sure they had gone away. At last she turned her head to one side, to ease the stiffness in her neck. Beside her she saw a line of tiny ants going in and out of a small crevice in the rock. Each little ant was carrying something . . . hurrying inside with a bit of straw or a wee bug. Coming out of the crevice, the ants carried white grubs. They were baby ants, Grandmother had told Moki once, being carried outside for an airing. Moki chuckled to see how much the ants looked like women carrying babies on their backs in cradleboards . . . I'll bet all those working ants are women ants, she told herself. The warrior ants must be off on a raiding party.

Watching the little ants, Moki fell asleep. When she awoke the sun was high overhead, blazing down without pity on the bare rocks about her. Her face felt fiery hot and her mouth as dry as an old piece of rawhide. For an instant she wondered where she was and what she was doing there. Then she remembered. She was thirsty, and hungry, too; but there was no food or water. She was there for a dreaming, and being hungry and thirsty was a part of it . . . But no dream had come to her as she slept. Perhaps she had not waited long enough, or the mai-yun did not like it that she had done this thing.

She raised her head and looked about her. The men were gone, and the buzzard no longer circled in the empty sky. Even the ants had stopped going in and out of the rock crevice. Her eyes ached from the sun's rays, glittering on the shiny rocks. For the first time since early morning, she thought of Little Wolf, her brother, wondering if he was as hot and thirsty and hungry as she was. Her father had spoken truly when he said, "This is no easy thing you seek to do, my son." It seemed a long, long time since she had sat beside the tipi, listening to words she knew she shouldn't hear.

Stiffly, Moki got to her feet and looked about for a bit of shade, but there was none. Only the sun-hot rocks and a few grayish weeds, with here and there a scrawny bush not big enough to shade even a rabbit.

A rabbit! Moki's hand flew to her mouth. Her rabbit! Had she given him his food and water this morning? She screwed up her eyes and thought hard, trying to remember. There had been breakfast, and she had helped tidy up the beds, and then her mother had gone to a friend's tipi . . . Ha-Co-Dah had gone over to watch the older boys shoot at marks . . . No, she could not remember giving her pet any food. Poor Rabbit! How hungry and thirsty he must be by now . . . Perhaps Ha-Co-Dah had fed and watered him.

But Moki knew better than that. Ha-Co-Dah liked to pretend to feed and water his stick horse, but he would never think to take care of Moki's rabbit.

Of a sudden she wanted to run down the hill and back to camp to take care of him, but she thought, No, I came here for a dreaming. I will not think of anything else. Perhaps the vision will come soon. Then I can go home and give Rabbit a drink . . . and have one myself, too. Strongly, she put the thought of her rabbit and of a cool drink of water away from her, trying to keep her mind blank so that she could receive any message or vision that the mai-yun might send to her.

The hot afternoon stretched on and on. It was the longest day she had ever known. Almost the sun seemed to stand still in the sky, pouring down on her like white-hot rain. She put her hands over her face to shield her eyes from the rays of the sun, but even then there was still a red-burning, though her fingers felt a little cool to her hot cheeks for just an instant. She was so thirsty.

The dusty, hot smell of the rocks and the gray-burnt weeds was strong in her nostrils. Absently, she picked a leaf from a scrawny bush and crushed it in her fingers. Its smell was sharp and bitter, bringing welcome water to her gritty-dry eyes.

Slowly she rubbed her fingers in the sand to rid them of the stinging tang of the leaf.

In spite of herself, thoughts swarmed into Moki's mind. Thoughts of the camp . . . of her mother, wondering where she, Moki, was. Worrying about her . . . Thoughts of Ha-Co-Dah . . . who would be looking after the small brother? . . . Moki squirmed miserably, knowing that she was causing trouble at home. Thoughts of the other children playing . . . Perhaps they were at the creek. Almost her thirsty skin could feel the soft wetness of the water . . . so cool . . . so cool.

With an effort, Moki brought her mind back to her purpose in being out here on this rocky hill in the burning sun. She was doing a big thing! No other Cheyenne girl ever had gone out to seek a vision . . . She would be honored. Her father would have pride in her . . . Thinking, she dozed, and woke, and dozed again in the heat, but still the mai-yun sent her no message.

After forever and forever, the evening came across the prairie. Far away a dust cloud rose. Moki knew it was the horse herd being brought in close to camp for the night. She could hear, or did she only imagine she heard, the whoops of the boys racing the frisky horses whose sides were round from feeding all day on the good strong grass.

The sun reached the edge of the earth and hid his burning face behind a dark-gray cloud bank, shooting bright golden rays up into the sky from behind the high-piled thunderheads. Darkness came on quickly, and the night air was still and hot as midsummer. Not the slightest breeze came to lift the sweat-sticky hair from Moki's forehead. The rocks around her were as hot, almost, as those heated in a fire to drop into a skin-kettle to cook soup.

Soup! Moki's stomach twisted with hunger. She tried to swallow and her throat seemed to stick together with the dryness. Darkness was thick all about her now, and overhead the stars were coming out. How far away they were tonight, dim and somehow cold-looking. Moki thought of her friend and searched the sky for the star person who had twinkled at her so many nights as she lay in her own bed, but without the tall tree beside the home tipi to point the way for her looking she could not find her friend.

In some special way, not finding her star made Moki feel even more lonely than she had before, all day out there on that rocky hilltop, waiting for a dreaming that never came . . . that she felt sure, now, would never come, because what she was doing was a thing she should not do . . . a wrong thing, that could only bring evil and never good.

She bit her quivering lip and blinked back the water in her eyes that blurred out the dim starlight. As she moved a little, the scrape of her buckskin dress against a dry weedstalk was loud in the stillness. Alone in the big dark, Moki was miserable and afraid. If only she had not come to this faraway high hill . . . if she had closed her ears to the words she should not have heard! Little Wolf was alone, too, out there somewhere in the dark. He was hungry and thirsty, too, waiting for a dreaming; but he would not be afraid . . . not the brave Little Wolf.

He was tall, almost a young warrior . . . and she was small, and a girl, and the fear was strong in her. A scurrying noise of some creature running startled her. Out on the prairie a coyote yammered, then broke into a hungry howl. Remembering the fierce yellow eyes and the slavering jaws of the coyote at the spring, Moki wedged herself as close as she could into a crevice in the rocks. She tried to tell herself that it was the same darkness that came every night to cover the prairie so the night animals could hunt for food and the day animals could sleep. But it didn't seem the same, out here alone. She clamped her hands over her ears to shut out the scary sounds, but her eyes kept darting here and there, trying to see what terrible things were lurking in the night.

The cloud bank in the south and west built higher and higher against the stars. Lightning flickered and flickered like the light of a campfire on a tipi wall. Thunder muttered and grumbled. The clouds boiled higher, and streaks of lightning split the sky, making the prairie white like moonlight, leaving it dark again as Thunder spoke in a great loud voice.

A wild, gusty wind came tearing along, swooping up sand and twigs and leaves, throwing them into Moki's face, whipping her hair into her eyes. She struggled to her feet and faced the storm while the wind tore at her, making a coldness where her sweat-damp dress touched her skin. Lightning darts flew faster and faster, cracking like whips, and Thunder boomed louder than any noise she had ever heard in all her life.

Was it that the mai-yun were so terribly angry that she, a little girl, had dared to seek a dreaming? There was a shaking of great fear inside her, and she cried out, staring wildly up into the tumbling storm clouds, "Have pity on me, Spirits-Who-Rule-the-Earth! Have pity!" but the wind tore her words away and flung them down over the prairie. There came no answer but the howling wind and the crackling lightning.

It was then she saw it. In one small space between the twisting angry clouds she saw it . . . the star-person, her friend, looking down. The clouds swept over it before she could call out, but it had been there. She saw it . . . then it was gone.

Now she felt truly lost and alone, sure that the brave deed she had tried to do was not brave, but foolish. She was a girl, just a little girl, and the mai-yun were angry that she had dared so greatly. A strong terror gripped her and she ran headlong down the hillside, stumbling, falling, picking herself up

. . . crying from the hurting and the fear. Constantly flashing lightning made a brightness all about her, showing her strange and terrifying shapes of things moving in the storm.

Half blinded by the slashing rain, Moki ran into something . . . some great beast . . . It plunged, squealing. Moki slipped in the mud, trying to run from the horsemen revealed by the lightning. One leaped from his horse and grabbed her, holding her fast as she fought to get away.

"What is it, Magpie?" another horseman shouted. "What scared your horse? Is it some animal?"

Moki went limp with relief. These riders in the storm could have been an enemy war party, but the words were Cheyenne and Magpie was a man from her own village.

He held her off to look at her by the flashes of lightning. "Why, it's a child . . . a girl child!" he cried. Startled words came from the others, riding in close, "Who are you, small one? What are you doing out here in the dark and storm alone?"

Moki couldn't answer. She could only huddle against the ground in the pouring rain, looking up at the men, so tall and strange in the glare of the lightning. The man whose horse had shied gathered her in his arms and handed her up to one of the other riders.

Back at the camp the horsemen answered the challenge of the watchers. All the tipis were tight shut against the storm, with only a few camp dogs to run out and give them a noisy greeting. The man carrying Moki took her, shivering, into his own tipi, laying her gently on a bed beside the small, clear-burning fire.

When Moki saw the man's wife hoist her great bulk to come and see what he had brought in, she felt great relief. She had been brought to the tipi of Two Crows, the mother of Spotted Fawn, and she knew that her own home was just across the camp circle.

Two Crows made small clucking sounds as she rubbed Moki's cold feet and wrapped her in a dry, warm robe. As soon as her husband had eaten he left the tipi, and in only a little while Moki's father came stooping through the tipi door. His face was very grave as he thanked Horse Running, the husband of Two Crows. "You have made our hearts glad, my friend, in bringing back the small one."

Horse Running waved a hand. "It is nothing, my friend. Children often stray too far from home."

But Moki knew that she had shamed her father before them all . . . that Cheyenne girls did not stray "too far from home" . . . and the talking of Two Crows was like the constant flowing of a river. With the morning, all the camp would know that the small daughter of Red Wolf had been found far out on the prairie, alone in the night. Her name would be spoken in the camp, but it was a speaking to bring shame, not pride, to her father.

At home there were her mother's gentle hands, and her own soft bed, and no word of scolding from her father, but only the question, "Why did you go out alone, Little Woman? We have searched and searched for you."

She covered her face with her hands, to hide the tears running. It was hard to tell, this foolish thing she had tried to do . . . "I . . . I went out to a high place for a dreaming."

She heard her mother's quick-drawn breath and her father move, startled. His voice was stern when he spoke, at last. "A dreaming is not for a little girl, my daughter. A dreaming is for one who would be brave and have a heart strong to face the enemy in battle . . . for one who would be wise to follow the right road. It is a hard thing, and not every one who goes out into the hills is given a vision."

There was a silence, then. She wanted to cry out, But I wanted to be brave, my father! But the words would not be spoken.

In the stillness she could hear the small scrape of his moccasins as he got up, and his voice was different, somehow, and kinder. "A woman's heart can be strong without a dreaming, my daughter. Leave men's ways to men . . . Let there be no more going out on the prairie alone. I have spoken."

MOKI WOKE the next morning with a hurting in her throat, and a burning fever that kept things hazy in her mind. Grandmother gave her a bitter medicine tea, and put a poultice of pounded leaves on her throat.

By the time that Little Wolf came back from his starving time, three suns later, Moki was feeling better. Little Wolf looked different, though . . . taller, and thinner. But most of all there was a different look to his face . . . the look of one who has suffered and is the stronger for the suffering.

There was no talk in the tipi about his going out, and no mention again of the thing Moki had tried to

114

do. While she was sick, Hogea came to the lodge to ask about her, and Mother Running Deer said only that Moki had a sore throat, and nothing of why she had it.

Then there came a day when Hogea and Antelope Girl and some others came by with their dogs hauling loaded travois, just like the pony drags that hauled camp gear when the Cheyennes moved from one camp site to another.

"Come on, Moki," Hogea called out to her. "You're well now. Your mother says so, so get your things together. We're all going out to make a play-village."

"I'll have to take Ha-Co-Dah," Moki said.

Antelope Girl lifted one shoulder and turned her lips down. "That's not a new thing. You always have to take Ha-Co-Dah, wherever you go. I'm glad I don't have a little brother to take care of all the time, aren't you, Hogea?"

Hogea shook her head, hard. "No, I'm not. I think a small person to live in our lodge would be fun . . . I'll tell you what, Moki. Today, let Little Grasshopper live in my tipi. I'll look after him and be his mother."

While they waited, Moki quickly packed her play tipi, made of hides too old and worn to use for real lodge coverings, and all her playthings, and fastened them to the two poles tied to Old One Eye, the biggest of their dogs. An old dog was best for packing, for a young one sometimes got excited and ran off after a rabbit or a squirrel, scattering camp gear all over the prairie.

Just before she left, Moki ran to give her rabbit fresh grass and cool water. She moved his willow cage over so that the hot sun would not get on it later in the day. Watching his nose twitch and his lips wiggle as he munched the green grass, Moki laughed.

"Don't gobble so, my good friend," she said. "No one will take your food away from you. You just take your time and chew it well. That way you will get the strength from it . . . that's what our mother is always telling my small brother . . . He's a fast eater, too, you know."

The rabbit twitched his long ears to show he was listening, and went on eating, watching her out of his bright, round eyes.

"Hurry, Moki! We can't wait all day for you to play with that silly rabbit of yours." Moki didn't have to look around to know how Antelope Girl's lip was curling.

He's not a silly rabbit, Moki said to herself fiercely. He's a Rabbit-person, and he loves me! I wouldn't let anything hurt him. Not anything! But she didn't want to be left behind, so she scratched Rabbit's head, and ran away to catch up with the others moving out to their camp ground, Ha-Co-Dah trotting along with her on his stick horse.

When the play-tipis were set up in a proper camp circle, the boys chose the girls to be their wives and the little children chose their mothers. Ha-Co-Dah chose Hogea as his mother, and went to live in her lodge. For that day, he was her child and she would look after him. Moki and her play-husband were chosen by two little girls, Bluebird and Shell. They were sisters, and the small one, Shell, could barely walk. She toddled about on her short fat legs, keeping as close to her sister as a noonday shadow.

While the girls were setting up their housekeeping things, the boys divided into soldier bands. Holding a tribal council, they elected Turtle as chief. He named the Dog Soldier band as camp guards and police, and sent the Kit Fox and the Elk bands out to scout for meat. As soon as they had gone the rest of the boys set to work making spears out of tall, stiff weeds, or checking their bows and arrows.

Moki took her two small girls and went with a party of other camp mothers out across the prairie to dig roots. They were fortunate. They found a place where many wild turnips grew. Fat little Shell prodded in the dirt with her short root digger, grunting and puffing, but getting very few turnips to show for all her work.

The older little girl did better with the digging, getting a nice bunch of turnips for the cooking pot. "You have done well, small daughter," Moki said, putting the turnips in the sack she carried.

Bluebird smiled, ducking her head shyly. Little Shell pulled at Moki's skirt. "Shell dig turnip too! Next time Shell dig many turnips." Moki patted her head, smiling at her boasting.

As they were going back to camp, they met Hogea and some of the others coming in with loads of wood on their backs, tied with tumplines across their foreheads. Two of the hunters brought in a ground hog they had trapped, and some other boys brought birds and rabbits they had shot. Soon the cooking fires were going and a good, rich smell of roasting meat brought the camp warriors from their spear-throwing, but as soon as they had eaten they went back to their contests.

Spear-throwing and arrow-shooting were more than games to Cheyenne boys. They were a most important part of their training to become men, brave and skillful warriors. Even the tiniest boys tried to see who could throw his sharpened stick farthest, and older boys delighted in hurling their spears and shooting their arrows at moving targets.

It was a great day for a small boy when he killed his first rabbit with his spear or arrow. Ha-Co-Dah had not yet brought down any game, but he practiced hard every day. The trouble was that the rabbit wouldn't stand still long enough for him to hit it. Always, it was off with a flash of its white tail, and Ha-Co-Dah's spear landed where the rabbit

118

had *been*, not where it was. His play-father watched him throwing.

"My son," he said, at last, kindly, "you must do one of two things. You must throw your spear much faster, or you must throw ahead of the rabbit so that your spear will be there to meet him."

Ha-Co-Dah looked puzzled. "But how do you know which way a rabbit will be going, so you can throw ahead of it?" he asked. "I've watched rabbits running in a path like that of the Summer lightning . . . and out of sight nearly as quickly . . . It would be better, I think, to throw faster and to try to get closer to the rabbit before I throw . . . I will try that, I think."

The older boys were choosing up sides for a game of war. One group would be Crow warriors and attack. The others would defend the village, throwing up breastworks and setting up defensive lines to protect the play-camp.

Some of the girls set to work dressing out the skins of the small animals the boys had taken during the morning. They staked out and scraped each tiny skin just as carefully as if it were the hide of a great buffalo bull. These would be tanned and used for robes for babies and many other things where softness and warmth were more important than strength and toughness.

Moki had a rabbit skin that was already tanned, so

she got out her little rawhide kit of sewing tools and sinew. She wanted to make a doll for her play-child, little Shell, sleeping now in their tipi. Blue-bird sat quietly beside Moki, her dark eyes intent, watching her play-mother's slim brown hands move in and out as she threaded the tough sinew through tiny slits in the soft skin.

"Will it be a boy doll or a girl doll?" the small one asked.

Moki looked up from her sewing at the round little face, the great dark eyes, the long black braids tied with deerskin thongs. It was as if she saw her-self, five summers ago, watching her mother making a robe for the baby she said would be coming to live with them. She had asked her mother, then, "Will it be a boy baby or a girl baby?"

Moki had held her breath, waiting for the answer. She did want a baby sister so much! Her mother had said, smiling, "Perhaps a girl, perhaps a boy . . . it will be as the mai-yun will it." But the baby that had come had been Ha-Co-Dah, a lively little grass-hopper of a boy. She remembered how happy her mother had been . . . how proud her father was of his second son.

Now Moki answered the small one. "It will be a boy doll, of course. Nobody wants a girl doll."

Bluebird got up and walked slowly away. Moki remembered the lonely time when Mother and Grandmother were so busy with the new baby.

120

They didn't have time to brush Moki's hair or tell her stories. There were presents for the new boy baby, but no presents for Moki. There was a great feast and the oldest Wise One pierced the tiny boy's ears and gave him a name . . . and a small girl stood about unnoticed at the edge of the crowd, watching.

Moki shook her head, putting the memories out of her mind, and went back to her sewing. Soon the little doll was all finished. She called Bluebird. "Come, my daughter, we must gather milkweed fluff to fill our doll. If we hurry we can get it stuffed before your sister wakes. Won't it be fun to watch her when she sees her new dolly?"

Bluebird brought another little girl along. In almost no time at all they had plenty of soft, fluffy milkweed down, and Moki tucked it carefully into every part of the doll's body, padding out the legs, arms and head. Now he wore only a breechclout, but next time Moki would make him some moccasins and a proper robe.

The sun was still high, but a white quarter moon showed in the east, pale against the blue of the sky. Now the game of war began. The Dog Soldier band, named by Turtle as play-camp guards, had scouts posted. One came running into camp to report to Turtle and his war chief.

"There's a strong force of Crow warriors headed this way! They come from the north. They have many horses, and every man is painted for war!"

The Cheyenne camp was thrown into an uproar. The main body of young warriors had marched out, earlier, to the west. Hastily, the War Chief sent runners out to find them and tell them of the danger to the camp. Soon they were streaming back into the village. They had been hunting the make-believe Crow group who had left the camp and circled back to attack from the north. Now they would have a grand battle. The boys were prancing with excitement.

The War Chief issued his orders in a loud voice. "Women, get yourselves ready to run. You six take the children and the pack dogs into that ravine to the south. The rest of you make weapons. Men, get ready to fight. Set up three lines of defense. Don't shoot until the enemy is near enough to hit . . . now, to your places!"

The War Chief was in complete command. Everyone hurried to follow his orders. The girls took down their little lodges and loaded their travois. The boys took up their limber throwing sticks, loaded with mudballs. Most of the girls were making more mudballs, but Moki was one of those named to go with the children and the pack dogs, into the ravine. Part of the Dog Soldiers were set as a guard over them. These would take no part in the fighting unless the enemy broke through the other defenses. Then they would fight a rear-guard action to cover their families as they ran away.

Scouts kept hurrying in to report to the War Chief. "The enemy is getting closer!" "The Crows are sending some warriors around to the east, to come in at the upper end of the valley."

The War Chief talked briefly with the council, drawing lines on the ground with a stick. One member of the council made a drawing of his own. They studied both drawings carefully, then the War Chief nodded his head, and added a mark or two to his own plan of action. There was a general agreement among the council, and the War Chief swung part of his forces to meet the attack coming from the east.

In the ravine, Moki and the other girls had their hands full with the dogs and the little children. They were as excited as if this had been a real attack by real enemies of the Cheyennes instead of a play-battle. Little boys, too young to be chosen for the soldier bands, shook their spears and made big talk about what they would do when the enemy came.

One of these was Ha-Co-Dah, astride his stick horse, spear in hand. Tiny girls clutched their dolls, huddled in tight little groups. Seeing them, Moki suddenly remembered her play-children, the two small sisters . . . she hadn't seen them since the war scare started. She should have brought them into the ravine for safety . . . but surely they had come in with the others!

Moki stopped Hogea. "Have you seen Bluebird and little Shell?" she asked.

"Bluebird is over there by that big rock." Hogea pointed up the ravine. "But I haven't seen Shell since the sun was nearly overhead."

Moki ran to see for herself. Sure enough, Bluebird was there with the others, but Shell was not there. Alarmed, now, Moki hurried from group to group, calling out the little one's name, Bluebird trailing after her, an anxious frown on her little face. They looked all among the children, the cluster of pack dogs, and behind every cedar bush . . . but they could not find the child.

Moki asked everyone she met, "Have you seen the small one? . . . Have you seen little Shell?" And everywhere she went the answer was the same, no one had seen her . . . no one knew where she was.

Everyone said she would be all right, but Moki had to know! Little Shell was her baby, her responsibility. If anything bad happened to her . . .

At the thought of danger to Shell, Moki began climbing the steep wall of the ravine. She had to get out of there and find the small one! But the Dog Soldier guards made her turn back.

"The Crows will take you," they said. "The child is hidden away somewhere. She'll be safe enough. You stay here with the other women and children so we can protect you." There was nothing for Moki to do but to stay there, but she kept looking and looking for little Shell.

At the camp site there was fierce fighting. The Crow warriors rushed, yelling, at the defenders. The Cheyennes fired at close range, scoring many hits with their mudballs. The enemy fell back, then rushed again. This time they came from the north and the east, too. Mudballs flew, but when the attackers got too close, the defenders dropped their limber throwing sticks and the warriors wrestled hand to hand.

The Crows broke through the first line, and the second line of defense bent under their fierce assault. The Dog Soldiers, guarding the ravine, ordered the girls to pick up their packs and the children who had to be carried and stand ready to run for safety. Moki took little Bluebird on her back, but she kept anxiously looking for the baby, Shell. She just had to be there somewhere in the crowd, but Moki couldn't find her, and little Bluebird kept saying, over and over, "I want my sister . . . where's my little sister?"

Now the third line of the Cheyenne defenders braced the second, and together they held firm. Rallying, the first-line warriors surrounded the enemy, and the battle was soon over, with many Crow warriors captured and horses taken. Coups were counted on the fallen enemy braves. The girls came out of the ravine, giving the victory trill and singing the strong heart songs, praising the fighting Cheyennes.

Only Moki and Bluebird did not join in the celebrating. They were searching for little Shell. She was not with the warrior bands. She was not among the captured enemy. Seeing Hogea, Moki called to her, "Will you help me, my friend? I must find my small daughter." For Moki, the fun was over. If any harm had come to baby Shell! . . . But where to look? Not to the north or the east. The Crow attackers had come from there. They would have taken her prisoner if they had found her.

The west? The main Cheyenne force had been called back from the west. If Shell had been out there they would have brought her in, as a straggler. So it was to the south that Moki and Hogea went, calling the small girl's name, climbing to every high spot to look out over the prairie for her. They had not gone too far when they saw two little girls coming. It was Shell and a larger child. But there was something wrong. Shell was leaning on the other girl, hobbling along slowly, using a stick as a brace.

Moki ran to her. Her little face was pale, her eyes wide with fear and pain. "What is the matter, my small one? What has hurt you?" Moki cried.

"A snake . . . a great big rattlesnake!" Tears ran down the little girl's cheeks and her voice quivered.

"We were digging turnips," the other child broke in. "I saw the snake, but he was striking already. I tried to kill him with my digger, but he crawled away . . . He was a very big snake."

On her knees now, Moki saw the fang marks on the small one's chubby ankle, just above her moccasin. "How long . . . how long ago did it happen?" She was getting the sharp cutting tool from her sewing kit. "Sit down, quickly! Let me get a cord around this leg."

"It was just a very little while ago," the other girl said. "We came as fast as we could . . . I couldn't carry her, she's too heavy . . . Will she die, Moki, do you think? Will the bite of the big snake kill her?"

Hogea was crying, but Moki had no time for tears. Already the little leg was beginning to swell. Quickly, she tied a thong from her hair around Shell's leg, just below the knee. "Hold it, Hogea. Hold it as tight as you can. Grandmother told me what to do for snakebites . . . I just hope it is not too late."

Two swift strokes with the sharp stone knife laid

the fang marks open. The tiny girl flinched, but did not make a sound, her big eyes fixed on Moki's face. Moki put her mouth to the wound and sucked as hard as she could. Again and again she sucked on the wound, spitting the poisoned blood on the ground. Its taste was sick in her mouth, but there was no time to think of that.

She had to get little Shell back home quickly. What she had done was just the first step. Only the Medicine Man had the power to cure a snakebite. With so much time already passed, it would take strong medicine to save the child. To the other little girl Moki said, "Run back to the play-camp and tell the chief, Turtle, what has happened. Tell him to send the fastest runner to our village to tell Shell's father. He will get the Medicine Man."

"Let me help you carry her," Hogea begged as Moki struggled to get Shell up. So they made a pack saddle of their linked arms and the little girl hung her arms around their necks, and they struck off straight across country to the home camp. The trip back was longer than it had seemed that morning. The sun had gone down before they came in sight of the camp circle. Shell's father, Buffalo Hump, came out to meet them. He took his little daughter from their tired arms and ran with her to the lodge of the Medicine Man.

There was a crowd gathered outside, but Moki and Hogea worked their way through to the doorway. A fire was burning inside the lodge, and it threw a flickering light over strange things.

Moki had never seen inside the Medicine Man's lodge before. Once she had kicked a ball against it. She had been terribly frightened, for something very bad could happen to anyone who disturbed the Medicine Man. She had waited, heart in mouth, but the Medicine Man had not come out, and after that she had stayed as far away from his tipi as she could.

Now she saw him, tall in the firelight. His face was painted, and he wore his medicine hat and carried his medicine shield. He shook his medicine rattle and sang his medicine songs of healing. Shell looked so very small, lying on a robe beside the fire. Her eyes were closed, and Moki was cold with fear.

Then the Medicine Man stopped singing and laid aside his rattle. Kneeling down, he moved his hands in a ceremonial way over the little girl. From a pouch he took something . . . Moki couldn't see what it was . . . and sprinkled it on the fire. It caused a whitish smoke to rise, and the Medicine Man passed his hands through the smoke four times.

His wife handed him a vessel of hot water, watching silently while he put something in it. With a horn spoon, he dipped water from the vessel and poured it on Shell's swollen leg. Four times he did this thing.

The little girl opened her eyes, then closed them

again. She looked so sick, so terribly sick. A little chill ran through Moki's body. She had never seen anyone look so sick before. Shivering, she looked at Buffalo Hump, Shell's father.

He knelt beside the sick child, not touching her but watching ever so intently. The old Medicine Man took up his rattle again and shook it very hard. He sang another song. A long silence filled the tipi when the song was ended. The Medicine Man stooped close to look into Shell's face. When he straightened up, he spoke to Buffalo Hump.

The warrior's face seemed to grow older. Slowly, slowly, he shook his head.

The old Medicine Man spoke again, more earnestly.

For an instant, Buffalo Hump's shoulders sagged. Then he got slowly to his feet and left the lodge, his face set and grim, and the silent, watching crowd outside opened to let him pass through.

Trembling, Moki watched him go. Then, swiftly she worked her way through the crowd again as they turned back to watch and wait at the lodge entrance. She had to follow . . . she had to know . . .

She came to where the tall warrior stood alone in the dim moonlight, his head bowed. What had the Medicine Man said to him that sent him out of the lodge into the night? Never had Moki spoken to a man of the village except her father and her grandfather, and the words she tried to speak now seemed stuck in her throat . . . but she had to know; fear for little Shell drove her to speak.

"What . . . what did the Medicine Man say to you?" The words sounded loud in the night, and Moki stopped short. She wanted to run away, but the tall warrior looked so . . . troubled. She could not see his face, but she could see his hands, tight clenched behind his back.

The father turned to look down at her. "Who is it who asks?"

Moki's voice came in a frightened whisper. "I am Moki. I found the small one and brought her home."

"My little daughter is close to death. The Medicine Man has sung his songs of healing, but there is no answer to his prayers."

"Oh!" Moki gasped. "Is there nothing more he can do? . . . The Medicine Man is very wise. My grandfather says his power is great. Is the power of the rattlesnake stronger than his?"

"It may be . . . it may be, this time." Buffalo Hump's voice was deep with pain. "The Wise One wants a rabbit . . . a young rabbit, alive, to kill and bind on the wound. The strong evil of the snake might go into it and leave my child in peace." The warrior's hands twisted. It was as if he struggled with something. "Oh, if it were only daylight. The night is no time for hunting . . . I cannot get him a rabbit!"

For an instant Moki stood still, looking at the dark ground under her feet, then she looked up past Buffalo Hump's bent shoulders to the stars.

There above the tallest pole of the Medicine Man's lodge, a small star seemed to wink. It was the star-person, the friendly star-person. It winked again, and again. It was like a message, telling her what she must do.

Quickly, she ran through the camp to their own tipi. The small willow cage still hung from the meat-drying rack where she had left it that morning, before they went out to make the play-village. The stars and the thin moon gave light enough for her hands to open the little gate. Rabbit gave a little cry as she picked him up, then settled down in her arms as she turned back to the Medicine Man's lodge. How soft and warm his fur felt! She hugged him close, blinking back the water in her eyes that made her stumble on the familiar path. Never had he seemed so dear . . . so helpless.

At the door of the lodge she stopped, afraid to go inside. Almost she turned back, clutching Rabbit to her heart. She wanted to run back home . . . to put him back in his little cage where nothing could hurt him.

A stick broke and the flaring firelight showed the old Medicine Man on his knees, face lifted, eyes closed. Watching, Moki saw his wife raise little Shell to give her something from a small cup. The small one's head fell to one side, as limp as a deer felled by a lance. The medicine spilled from her lips.

Moki forgot her fear . . . forgot, even, how much she loved Rabbit. Quickly she stepped through the door and thrust Rabbit into the Wise One's hands. Wide-eyed, he stood tall, holding Rabbit high.

Moki dropped to her knees and covered her face with her hands. She could not bear to watch.

A small sound came into the silence of the tipi. Then, after a time, the healing songs began again, and the clatter of the medicine rattle. Four songs the Medicine Man sang, and each song four times.

Again, a long silence. Moki could hear the sound of a stick being placed on the fire, and the sound of small movements in the tipi.

Then, when she felt she could not endure the waiting and the silence any longer, a hand clasped her shoulder and the gentle voice of the Wise One's wife spoke softly: "Find the child's father, now, my daughter. Tell him the small one will live!"

AFTER THE good warm feeling of
the telling, and when all the people had returned to
their homes, Moki went alone to her own lodge, and
the camp settled to the night's quiet at last. She lay
long awake, until the little thin moon went away,
and only the far-seen stars made a dim light. In her
heart was a gladness that the small one had escaped
the evil power of the snake, but sorrow too, because
of Rabbit, who had had to die that little Shell might
be healed.

Tears wet her pillow, in the knowing that never
again would Rabbit play about the tipi or come to
nibble the good grass from her fingers when she
called to him. He had been her dear Rabbit-person
and he had loved her . . . and she had promised
that never, never would she let anything hurt him
. . . The aching loneliness was heavy in the darkness of the night.

When the morning came, Moki's mother called to her, "Come, my daughter, get yourself up and dressed. It is time you were out of your bed. Already your brother has gone out to hunt. Come now, and I will brush your hair for you."

Moki sat up in bed and rubbed the sleep from her eyes, feeling somehow numb and still tired, as though she had not really rested in the night. Draggingly, she dressed herself and went out to the cooking place. Her mother gave her some breakfast, but Moki wasn't hungry.

"Eat something, Moki . . . Here, try this bit. I saved it for you." Mother Running Deer put an especially nice, tender piece of meat into Moki's bowl, but Moki just looked at it, without picking it up. After a little, her mother took the bowl and gave the food to Old One Eye, Ha-Co-Dah's dog.

"Why don't you go and find Hogea, my daughter? The girls will be planning some games," Running Deer said. "You'll feel better if you get out with your friends."

Moki shook her head. She didn't feel like playing. "I'll make the beds, Nah-koa."

Inside the tipi, she fluffed up the grass and tucked the skins under smoothly, but her thoughts were not on what she was doing. She was thinking of yesterday. It was her fault. If she had been more careful in watching her play-child, little Shell would not have wandered off. Then the snake would not have bitten the small one, and Rabbit would still be in his little cage. That was what made her feel so bad . . . She had been the mother, and she had not taken care of her child. Water from her eyes ran down her cheeks.

There was a noise outside the tipi. Quickly, Moki wiped her eyes as her father, Red Wolf, came stooping through the door.

"My daughter, the warrior Buffalo Hump is here. He wants to see you!"

Surprised and puzzled, Moki went outside, stopping short at the sight of a crowd of people in front of their lodge. Buffalo Hump stood there, tall in the sunshine. He spoke in a strong voice, so that all the people who were gathered there could hear: "Moki, Little Woman, I have come to tell you that because of you there is joy in my lodge." He swung his hand in a broad gesture, and pointed to an old man standing near, "In your honor and because my heart is glad that my small daughter now lives, I give these two good horses and this meat and these robes to this poor man. He will ride about the camp, calling out so that all may hear, that Moki, brave daughter of the warrior Red Wolf, has saved the life of Buffalo Hump's child."

Moki could not believe that she was hearing right. Her name was to be called out in the village, as if she had done a big thing. Shell was just a little child, and a girl, too. Yet her father was doing this thing to honor Moki, the one who had saved her.

But this could not be, for only the names of brave warriors, of men whose deeds were great, were called out for honor by the crier. Boys, too, when they killed their first buffalo . . . but never a girl.

But the old man mounted one of the horses and, leading the other, he rode about the camp and Moki could hear his voice, over and over, loud and strong, "I call out the name of Moki, daughter of the warrior Red Wolf. Moki it was who saved the life of the brave Buffalo Hump's daughter. Because the child lives, Buffalo Hump has given these two good horses to me, a poor man. I call out the name of Moki . . ."

People came out of their tipis to hear, and women made the trill of applause. It was what Moki had always wanted; it was what she had worked for, what she had done so many foolish things, man-things, to try to get . . . Why was she not happy, now? Why did it all mean nothing to her?

Miserably, she stood staring at the ground at Buffalo Hump's feet, listening as her father spoke the proper words of appreciation for the honor done his daughter, and not even the sound of quiet pride in his voice made her feel any better.

As soon as she could, Moki went back inside the tipi. She was sitting on her bed, leaning against the painted backrest, when Hogea and Antelope Girl came in.

Antelope Girl's eyes were shining. "Oh, Moki,

I think it is the most exciting thing I ever heard of! Aren't you proud to have your name called out like that, for all the people to hear?"

Moki rolled a bit of the fringe of her dress between her fingers. "I guess so . . . I don't know how I feel, really."

Hogea sat down beside her. "I'm sorry about your rabbit, Moki. I know how hard it was for you to give him up . . ."

Tears came into Moki's eyes, and she turned her face away so they would not see her cry.

But Antelope Girl was talking again. "Ho," she said, airily. "What's a rabbit! Moki can get another rabbit . . ."

Sudden anger dried the water in Moki's eyes. "I don't want another rabbit!" she cried. "I don't ever, ever want another rabbit as long as I live!"

Frowning at Antelope Girl, Hogea patted Moki's hand. "I know how you feel, my friend . . . but remember the small one and be glad." She stood up, pulling Moki to her feet. "Come on, now, let's go outside and find something to do."

Moki didn't want to go with them, but it was easier to go along than to explain why she didn't want to go. Outside, a group of children flocked around them, talking about what had happened, and their voices were like the sound of many birds when they gather to fly south before the coming of Winter Man. Forgetting Moki's angry words, earlier, Antelope Girl walked close beside her, arm in arm, eager to share in her glory.

The afternoon was long and the playing tiresome, even though Moki was always chosen first for the games. Finally she left the group, saying only, "It is time that I returned to help my mother." But back at the home tipi, she did not go inside. Instead she wandered around to the back where Rabbit's little willow cage still hung from the meat-drying rack, with its door half open.

Moki was just taking the cage down when Ha-Co-Dah came around the tipi. "Grandfather wants you, Moki," he said. "You are to come right away to their lodge."

Setting the cage down carefully, at the foot of the tree, Moki hurried to see what her grandfather wanted. The inside of the Old One's tipi was dark after the brightness of the sunshine, but as Moki's eyes adjusted to the dim light she saw Grandfather Gray Hawk sitting cross-legged at the back of the lodge, facing the small fire in the center.

Moki was surprised to see that he was dressed in his finest clothes, wearing his many-feathered warbonnet, and holding his medicine shield. It was as if he were dressed for a great ceremonial occasion. He looked very grand. Grandmother, too, was dressed in her finest buckskin dress, beautifully embroidered with many-colored quills.

As Moki stopped just inside the door, Grandfather motioned with his eagle-wing fan. "Come in, my granddaughter. Come closer, so that I can see you better."

Wondering, Moki came to stand before the old man. He motioned with his fan again, and she knelt beside the fire watching him. After a time he spoke.

"The name of our granddaughter has been called out in the camp circle. It is a thing that has never happened before in the memory of the oldest man. Never has a young girl received such honor among our people." The old warrior raised his medicine shield. "You have done well, my granddaughter."

Moki felt a surge of gladness at her grandfather's words. That Grandfather was truly proud of her eased a little the tight hurting that had held her all day. "Ha-ho, Nam-shin," she said, softly. "Thank you, my grandfather."

Grandmother Doll Woman gave a soft trill of applause, then stopped as Grandfather spoke again, his voice now solemn and stern.

"It was a brave thing you did," he said. "A good and womanly deed." He nodded his wise old head and the firelight glowed on the feathers of his headdress, each feather showing a coup he had counted, an honor earned. "It is as I have said before, a woman's heart is strong and brave for giving . . . and you, my granddaughter, have truly earned your name, Moki . . . Little Woman."

Moki could not speak for the lump in her throat.

She bowed her head, and there was silence for a time. Then she heard a rustling as Grandmother came to kneel beside her, placing in her hands a pair of moccasins, soft and white, beautiful with finest quilling.

"For you, Granddaughter," Doll Woman said, softly. "Put them on . . . and may they carry your feet in the right road."

Moki slipped her feet into the new moccasins. How beautiful they were, slender and small, and fitting so perfectly. "Nish-ki, my grandmother, I thank you!" she said. Then, "May I go now, please? I would show my fine new moccasins to my mother."

Grandfather Gray Hawk got to his feet. "Go now, my granddaughter, and try no more to walk in men's ways. You have found the moccasins to fit your feet."

Moki looked back from the door, raising a hand in salute to the tall old warrior whose feathered war-bonnet seemed almost to touch the top of the tipi. He smiled and a little of the cold loneliness went out of Moki's heart. But down deep there was still a hurting that not even Grandfather's approval could ease.

When Moki came to the cooking place, at home, Mother Running Deer was boiling meat and getting food ready for the evening meal. Her face was proud when Moki told her about Grandfather's words and Grandmother's gift of the fine moccasins. While Running Deer examined the quilling, Little Wolf came in from his hunt with a many-antlered deer slung over his horse. Quickly, Moki ran to hold his horse while he unloaded the deer, with the doubtful help of Ha-Co-Dah's pulling and hauling at its forefeet. It was a big deer, and fat.

Breathing hard from the lifting, Little Wolf said, "Tell our sister that she is to have the skin of this deer, for a new dress." He spoke to Ha-Co-Dah, though Moki was beside him, since it was not proper that he speak directly to her. "Tell her, too, that I have found a new pet for her." He reached into the small pouch he carried on his belt and brought out a small furry something.

Ha-Co-Dah took the little animal and put it in Moki's hands. Startled, she almost dropped it, for it was a tiny rabbit, smaller even than her dear Rabbit-person had been when Father Red Wolf had brought him to her in the moon when the leaves were new. But it was a rabbit, and the sight and feel of it brought the loss of her pet flooding back into her mind.

Forgetting for an instant what was fitting for her to do, she tried to thrust the little animal back into Little Wolf's hands, crying, "Take it back . . . I don't want it . . . I don't ever want another rabbit!"

144

Little Wolf's eyes widened. He backed away, not speaking, and it came to Moki, too late, that she had talked directly to her brother . . . that she had refused a gift. Shamed by her own rudeness, she ducked her head and ran away, still clutching the shivering little rabbit.

At the back of the tipi she threw herself on the earth under a tree, sobbing quietly. After a little the tiny rabbit squirmed and struggled in her hands. Wriggling, it poked its head between her fingers . . . stretched up to nuzzle her cheek, and the thought came to Moki, The poor little thing is hungry . . . it's afraid and it's hungry!

Wiping her eyes with a knuckle, she scrambled to her feet and ran to get water and some tender grass, muttering fiercely to herself as she ran, "It's not my Rabbit-person, and I'll never love it as I did him, but it's little and it needs me."

The baby rabbit chewed the grass greedily, its round eyes fixed on Moki, its ears laid down along its back. Of a sudden the little thing cowered against the ground, quivering, as Old One Eye, Ha-Co-Dah's big dog, came snuffling around the tipi.

In one movement, Moki scooped the frightened little rabbit up into her arms and threw a stick at the dog. "Get away from here! Get!" she stormed.

The old dog ran, yelping, but Moki knew he'd be back. The baby rabbit's life would be short, loose in the camp full of hungry dogs. The only place safe for the helpless little animal would be in a cage . . . Rabbit-person's cage.

For the barest instant, then, she hesitated, still not quite willing that even this warm, soft baby rabbit should have her old friend's home of woven willow.

Again the tiny rabbit nuzzled her cheek, trustingly.

It was too much. No matter what she had said before, Moki could not resist his helplessness. Holding him against her heart, she hung the little willow cage again on the drying rack and tucked the tiny rabbit safely inside. At first he huddled on the floor of the cage without moving, but in a little while one little ear twitched forward and the other back. His tiny nose began to wiggle.

Moki found herself smiling. He looked so funny! Speaking softly, she said, "Don't think I've forgotten you, dear Rabbit-person. I loved you, truly I did, and I'll never, never forget you . . . but this one is so little, and he has no one to take care of him but me. You'll not mind, now you're gone, if I let this small one have your home. For — " and now she laughed aloud, as all at once the heaviness left her heart at last. "For he's a little Rabbit-person too!"

ABOUT THE AUTHOR

Grace Jackson Penney spent her youth in Oklahoma, where she had many Native American friends and neighbors. As a journalist and newspaper correspondent, she published articles on a variety of subjects, and was especially interested in the history and folklore of Oklahoma and Native Americans.